Out of the Ashes

Danger in Destiny
Book 1

Melanie D. Snitker

DALLIONE MEDIA, LLC

Out of the Ashes
Danger in Destiny: Book 1
By Melanie D. Snitker

All rights reserved
© 2023 Melanie D. Snitker

Dallionz Media, LLC
P.O. Box 5283
Abilene, TX 79608

Cover Art: Dallionz Media, LLC

Editor: Krista Burdine at Grammaresque
https://iamgrammaresque.com/

For permission requests, please contact the author at the email below or through her website.

Melanie D. Snitker
melanie@melaniedsnitker.com
www.melaniedsnitker.com

This is a work of fiction. Names, characters, businesses, places, events, and incidents either are the products of the author's imagination or used in a fictitious manner. Any resemblance to actual persons, living or dead, or actual events is purely coincidental.

For James and Bev.
Your example of love and
dedication to each other
is truly an inspiration.
Love you both!

Chapter One

Smoke.

The faint smell made Megan Bristow sit up, her eyes bleary. She hadn't meant to fall asleep so quickly once she'd checked into her hotel room, but the long drive after coming off a twenty-four-hour shift at the hospital had caught up to her. She looked at her watch. It was just after ten o'clock in the evening.

She swung her legs over the side of the bed and sniffed the air. The hint of smoke was there, but barely. She leaned toward the nightstand. A quick inspection of the alarm clock and lamp cords assured her they weren't the source. The television and microwave seemed fine, too.

Megan went to the window and pulled back the beige curtains, half expecting to see the glow of a forest fire nearby that might account for the smell. The bright lights in her hotel room contrasted with the dark sky outside to create an almost ethereal reflection of herself. She cupped her hands around her face and leaned closer to the glass. From her vantage point on the third floor, she could see a smattering of cars in the parking lot below. Beyond that, shadows of trees reminded her the hotel was on the outskirts of her hometown of Destiny, Texas—a place she'd escaped from just days after her high school graduation.

She'd walked away from a messed-up home life. Those warm, fuzzy feelings you're supposed to get when you think of the place you grew up in? As far as Megan was concerned, they only existed in Hallmark movies and books. She wouldn't be back in Destiny nine years later if it weren't for her father's funeral tomorrow.

With any luck, she could attend the services and leave town again without running into too many people she used to know.

A weighted sigh escaped her lips and fogged the glass.

Another whiff of smoke reached her, and this time it was unmistakable. But where was it coming from? She pushed away from the window and yanked the curtains shut again. The rod that held them creaked its objection.

A fire alarm went off in the hallway, piercing the air with its urgency. The alarm in her room joined in, the bright, white light strobing against the drab walls.

Megan's heart lurched as she turned to look at the door of her hotel room. Thin wisps of smoke came in through the small space between the door and the floor, effectively eliminating any hope that it was an ill-timed drill.

Megan shoved her phone into her pocket, threw her purse over her shoulder, and glanced at the small suitcase that carried the rest of her belongings. She grabbed that, too, and dashed for the door.

Her mind racing, she instinctively reached for the doorknob to escape into the hallway. The moment her palm touched the metal, intense heat sent pain through her hand. She released the knob immediately, but not before it had already burned her. Megan hissed against the agony as she assessed the damage. Probably a second-degree burn.

So stupid! Of course, she should've felt the door first to make sure it wasn't too hot. How many times had she heard that in school as a child?

This meant the fire was in the hallway outside her room. She left the suitcase on the ground and ignored the pain pulsing through her hand. Megan raced to the bathroom, soaked a bath towel with water, and then shoved it against the base of the door. She whirled to face the window and pushed the curtains to the side. In moments, Megan had the window open, and the screen knocked out. She leaned over the edge and looked down.

A wrought iron ladder glinted in the moonlight. It was the nearly ancient kind that could extend downward to a platform on the second floor where another ladder would lead to the ground. Megan felt around the ladder for a switch or latch that would cause it to slide down. Nothing. The light outside was so low, it was impossible to see the release.

Sliding her purse straps to the elbow of her right arm, she dug around inside with her left hand until her fingers collided with the small, metal cylinder that had settled in the bottom.

Megan yanked it out, pushed the button on the back, and shined her flashlight down at the ladder. There! The latch slid to the side, but the ladder still refused to extend. She tossed the flashlight back into her purse, glancing again at the door as more smoke billowed in from around the edges. She eased herself up until she was sitting on the windowsill, then used one foot to push down on the ladder.

When that didn't work, she kicked it harder. Pain trav-

3

eled across the bottom of her foot, the sock she wore doing little to cushion the blows.

Urgency to escape her room threatened to morph into panic.

Megan took in several steadying breaths as she quickly thought through her options. This was not much different than dealing with an emergency at the hospital. She needed to think calmly, assess options, and come up with a plan.

Abandoning the window, she ran into the bathroom while she still could. After snatching a bath towel from the rack above the toilet, she got it wet under the faucet, then returned to the window.

This time, when she looked down, her gaze took in the lit parking lot three stories below. People milled about, some pointing at the building. Megan waved her hands back and forth. "Help me!" When a man looked up at her, she yelled again, "I'm trapped!"

The man cupped his hands around his mouth and called out, "The fire department is on the way."

Hopefully, help would arrive soon. In the meantime, Megan couldn't simply sit there and wait for the fire to eat through the door or wall of her hotel room. She wished she knew how bad the fire was in the hallway. Was it just outside her room? Or was the entire floor engulfed in flames? There was no way to know. She again leaned through the window and shook the fire escape ladder, willing it to finally lower like it was designed to do.

She'd seen some of her pediatric patients come into the hospital after being injured in a fire. The worst cases were horrifying, those images impossible to erase from Megan's mind. She would not be burned like that, even if it meant climbing down as far as she could and jumping to the platform below. A broken limb was, by far, the better choice.

Smoke seeped in all around the door and collected in billows against the ceiling. Even with the window open, the smoke made her nose run and her eyes sting. She coughed as she clutched the wet towel with her uninjured hand and brought it to her face.

Flames licked one corner of the door and worked their way upward, bringing with them a renewed sense of urgency.

Megan swallowed hard. She was going to be okay. She had to be. Destiny may have claimed her childhood and her illusions of a happy family, but she wasn't about to let it steal her life, too.

Sirens pierced the air, low at first, then louder as two fire engines pulled into the parking lot followed by an ambulance.

Megan breathed a sigh of relief, a feeling that didn't last long as the room behind her heated up. Sweat rolled down her back. She took the wet towel and draped it over her head, the cool fabric falling against her shirt.

She was vaguely aware of activity in the parking lot. The man who'd responded to her before waved a firefighter in her direction.

"God, please help me." The words barely reached her own ears.

The crackle of the fire was clear now, and it took everything in Megan to not turn and survey the room again. That wouldn't do any good. She'd either wait for someone to help her or jump and hope she aimed correctly for the little landing below.

The fire engine moved, and Megan watched as a ladder began to rise in her direction. Hope flared, and even though the ladder hadn't reached her yet, she eased closer to the edge of the windowsill.

A firefighter in uniform climbed the ladder. As he approached, he said, "Alright, we need to move quickly. Take my hand."

Familiarity teased her brain, but Megan didn't take the time to analyze it. She reached for him, welcoming the firm grasp as he eased her out of the window and onto the ladder in front of him. Once both feet and hands were secure on the rungs, he leaned forward to look at her face. "Are you injured?"

Megan blinked at him several times.

Perplexity, followed by recognition, filled his features.

It couldn't be.

But the piercing blue eyes, strong jaw, and timbre of his voice assured Megan that it was Bryce Keyes. The guy who'd stolen her heart in high school. It'd nearly killed her to walk away from him when she left Destiny.

Megan groaned and rested her forehead against a ladder rung as coughs wracked her body.

Bryce stared at Megan's profile. He had a million questions, but the sound of her coughing, plus the pop of the flames in the nearby hotel room, spurred him into action. "Can you climb down?"

She lifted her head from the ladder rung and glanced below them with a nod.

"Great. Slow and steady. I'm right here." They began their descent, his gloved hands on either side of her, penning her in with his arms to make sure she didn't fall. She moved along with him, gripping the ladder tightly with her left hand and gingerly with her right. Had she injured it? With only socks on her feet, Bryce knew the metal rungs of the ladder might be painful, but she didn't complain as she followed his lead.

When he stepped to the ground, he reached for Megan and helped her down the rest of the way. Together, they looked to the third story where flames extended through the window, a fiery contrast against the night sky. Bryce's heart pounded. That was much closer than he would've liked. He sent a silent prayer of thanks that he'd been able to get to Megan in time.

His fellow firefighters went into action to douse the flames before the fire spread to more of the hotel. He needed to help them, but first he had to make sure Megan was okay.

Without asking permission, he took her right hand in his and turned it over. The red flesh of her palm was already blistering. Bryce glanced around the perimeter of the crowd until he spotted an ambulance. As soon as the EMT stepped out, Bryce recognized his friend and waved him over, "Curtis! We've got a second-degree burn here. Possible smoke inhalation."

Curtis Whitman gave him a nod, grabbed a medical kit from the back of the truck, and headed their way.

Bryce turned his attention back to Megan. "Will you be okay?"

Sweat caused strands of light brown hair to cling to her flushed cheeks. She withdrew her injured hand from his and cradled it against her chest. But despite everything she'd been through, she stood tall, her back straight and chin lifted. "I'll be fine. Thank you."

He wanted to stay with her, but Deputy Chief Menendez caught his attention. "Keyes, I need you on the hose."

"Yes, sir." Bryce adjusted his gloves and looked Megan

in the eyes. "I'll find you later. Curtis will take good care of you."

She nodded.

With that, he turned away from her and focused on helping to douse the fire as some of the crew entered the building. While they battled the fire, he fought against thoughts of his ex-girlfriend. And failed miserably.

Megan was back.

Bryce had wondered if she might return for her father's funeral, but even then, he wasn't sure. Two days after they graduated from high school, she'd fled Destiny, and as far as he knew, she never gave the town—or Bryce—a second thought.

It would be easier if he could say the same thing about her. They used to talk about getting married after college. Building a life together. All of their plans evaporated right before his eyes. He tried to get hold of her, but she never returned his calls.

He spent months half expecting her to waltz back into town. Even longer trying to forget her, something that proved impossible.

Bryce moved on with his life—he had no choice. And while his relationships since then hadn't proven all that successful, he loved Destiny and the life he built. Yet, through it all, he'd always wondered what happened to the hazel-eyed beauty who had once stolen his heart. Who, if he was honest with himself, still held a piece of it hostage.

Seeing her here brought up a whole mess of emotions, questions, and memories he couldn't afford to focus on now.

The fire department and volunteers worked seamlessly to put the fire out. They managed to save the structure itself, but there was no way it would reopen soon. He didn't envy the hotel owners and the task they had ahead of them when it came to repairs.

All the guests would have to be relocated to one of the other hotels farther into town. It was Friday night, and the town's biannual Trade Days was going on. No doubt available hotel rooms would be hard to come by.

Bryce took his helmet off and swiped his arm across his forehead. He glanced around the parking lot before looking at his watch. It was Saturday now—nearly one in the morning. The end of September was the time of the year in Texas when morning temperatures started in the 60s but could rise to the 90s by midafternoon.

Deputy Chief Menendez stopped beside him and clapped him on the shoulder. "Nice work, Keyes." The words were spoken sincerely, but concern etched lines along the corners of his mouth. "A full investigation will be conducted. I thought you'd like to know that the fire originated in the hallway outside of the room where that girl you rescued was staying. It was set in a trash can, and an accelerant was used. I spoke with the hotel manager, and trash cans aren't normally in the hallways since each room contains several of their own."

Someone had purposefully relocated it. "Arson." It wasn't unheard of, but the motivation bothered Bryce. His eyes narrowed as he studied his friend and mentor. "Any idea why?"

Menendez shrugged. "It's impossible to know right now. I've got a call in to the police department. They are sending someone shortly to investigate. We took a quick look at the escape ladder since we got a report the occupant couldn't get it to work." He paused. "It'd been ziptied into place to prevent it from lowering. We're still checking the rest of the building, but it looks like the same was done to the ladders in multiple locations."

The evil things that some people did to others never ceased to amaze and sicken Bryce. Disbelief gave way to anger. "Megan nearly didn't get out in time. Whoever did this is lucky there were no casualties."

"We'll see what the investigations reveal. Maybe they've had problems with a guest who decided to lodge a more public complaint." Menendez looked grim. "I take it you and Megan know each other?"

"We were friends in high school. I hadn't seen her in years before tonight, though."

"I'll drive you to the station so you can get your truck. You should go by the hospital and check on her. Return to finish your shift once you have her settled. Let me know if you need anything."

"Thank you, sir." Bryce shook the deputy chief's hand. "I appreciate it."

On their way back, Bryce couldn't erase the image of Megan trapped in her room. Had the arsonist picked a random location to start the fire? Or had he specifically chosen that floor, or even the room, that Megan was staying in? His body tensed at the thought.

She was more than likely in the wrong place at the wrong time.

And it'd nearly gotten her killed.

Chapter Two

Bryce approached the treatment room at Destiny Community Hospital and paused in the doorway. Megan was listening to a woman dressed in scrubs.

"Since you're a nurse, too, I'm sure you don't need me to tell you how to treat your hand. But I'll put the instructions in here"—the nurse lifted a white plastic bag with handles—"along with the bandages and gauze. Keep an eye on it, though, and be sure to see a doctor if it looks like the wound is getting infected."

"I will. Thank you."

"Let me get one last O2 check on you quick..." The nurse put a pulse oximeter on Megan's finger. Both waited silently for the readings before she removed it again. "It looks good." The nurse gave a satisfied nod and tapped out the results on her iPad. "I'll go grab those discharge papers, and you'll be ready to go."

"I appreciate it." Megan stood from the hospital bed where she'd been sitting and cautiously flexed the fingers of her injured hand. She winced slightly before glancing up and spotting Bryce in the doorway. Her eyes widened for a moment as she cleared her throat. "Don't you have a fire to put out or something?"

Bryce chuckled as he stepped farther into the room. He took in Megan, the dirty smudges on her face, and the way her hair still hung in mild disarray. He'd often wondered how she might have changed over the last nine years. Goodness knew time had done a number on him, and not always in a positive way.

Looking at her now, she was the same woman. Sure, her face had filled out, her curves were more pronounced, and there were adorable little wrinkles at the corners of her eyes when she was smiling at the nurse a few minutes ago. Truthfully, she was even more beautiful now than she'd been back in high school. Attraction thrummed, and his gaze connected with hers.

She raised an eyebrow in response to his not-so-subtle scrutiny. Her hazel eyes looked more brown than green thanks to the tan shirt she was wearing.

"It's good to see you, Megan. You look great."

She shot him a dubious look. "After everything tonight, I know you're lying. Thank you, though. And it's good to see you, too." Megan lifted her bandaged hand. "If it weren't for you, this would have been the least of my worries."

Did she realize just how close she'd come to losing her life? Menendez's words flashed through Bryce's mind. He didn't see any reason to tell her about the arsonist when they had so little to go on. Instead, he focused on what brought her back to town. "I was sorry to hear about your father."

She glanced toward the door where the nurse exited earlier. "Thank you," she said softly. "I haven't been by the house yet. I figured I would check on Mom later this morning."

Bryce knew she and her parents hadn't been close while she was growing up, and the distance between them seemed to increase after leaving home. Had she seen her mom at all since then? "You might think about staying with your mom while you're here."

"No." The answer was immediately accompanied by a stubborn lift of her chin. "I managed to get my purse out with me." She tilted her head toward the small leather satchel on a chair nearby. "I can pay for a hotel. As for my outfit..."

Bryce took in her stocking feet. "You're going to need some shoes. Not to mention a change of clothes." He took a dramatic whiff of the air. "I'm not sure which of us smells more like smoke."

That coaxed a little smile. "I'm not sure, either."

"Unfortunately, Trade Days is this weekend. The hotels were full before the fire. So, if your mom's house is out, we're going to need to find you somewhere else to crash."

Megan shuffled her feet, her frown returning.

"Hold on, I may have an idea." He pulled his phone out and shot a text to his sister. Bryce smiled when he read Erica's response. "Erica owns a B & B now. She said she has a room—I'll give you a ride over there."

"I appreciate the offer, Bryce, but I'm going to need my car."

"Then I'll take you to the hotel where you can pick it up and follow me to the B & B." It seemed like the perfect solution. Maybe he was being overprotective, but he wanted to make sure she arrived at the B&B safe and sound before he returned to the station for the last few hours of his shift.

Megan's nose wrinkled, and that movement grabbed Bryce and dragged him straight into the past.

How many times had he seen her wrinkle her nose when she heard or saw something she didn't like? Back in high school, he'd found it adorable and would often kiss her nose in response. It'd been one of the fastest ways to turn her frown into a smile.

How had he forgotten all about that? Memories of time spent holding her in his arms, kissing her nose and then her lips, flooded his brain. It made him long for what used to be.

Except she was the one who chose to walk away. A lot changed in nine years—they were practically strangers now.

The reminder sobered his mood.

She must have sensed the change because her own expression softened. "That sounds great. Thank you again."

Bryce studied Megan as the nurse came back in and handed over the discharge papers.

"Don't forget what I said. If you ever decide to move back, we are always hiring." The nurse laughed good-naturedly before bustling out of the room.

Megan folded and tucked the discharge papers into her purse. Soot smudged her face, and her eyes drooped in a way that spoke of lack of sleep, and probably for longer than just last night.

"You work as a nurse?" Bryce led the way through the hospital and into the parking lot illuminated by tall streetlights.

"In the children's ward at a hospital in San Antonio." She didn't elaborate, but there was no missing the affection in her voice. Once they got settled in his truck, Megan set her purse on the floorboard near her feet and relaxed into the passenger seat. "So, Erica owns a B & B? Good for her."

Megan sounded surprised. Of course, when she last

knew Erica, his big sister had been on the wrong path. Erica was three years older than Megan and Bryce, but it took her a while to find her footing in life. "She had a rough time for several years. I mean, she wasn't doing great in high school, but she really struggled afterward. Her self-esteem was terrible." Bryce shook his head. He and his parents didn't know how to reach her back then. "She got married a few months after you left. To some guy she barely knew."

"Wow." Megan brushed some hair out of her face and then leaned her right elbow against the base of the window. "But she's okay now?"

"She is. She dealt with a messy divorce and is parenting a son on her own. But she's got her life figured out." It was true, too. Despite everything she'd been through, Erica had pulled things together. He was proud of her.

"Well, she has an amazing family who's got her back. That counts for a lot." Her voice sounded wistful. Was there a tinge of bitterness there, too? Maybe. The difference in their families was sometimes a source of tension between them back in the day. She'd been adamant about him not spending more time than necessary with hers.

"That she does." He turned into the hotel parking lot, his eyes drawn to the area of the third floor that had been damaged by the fire. It looked vacant—almost dead. A shiver of unease traveled up his spine. Everything could have ended so differently. If he hadn't gotten to Megan in time... He shoved that line of thought out of his head before he could finish it. She was okay, and there was no sense in dwelling on the alternative. *Thank you, Lord, for keeping her safe.*

Megan directed him to her car, and he parked in the space beside it.

"Just follow me, and we'll have you there and settled before you know it."

Less than ten minutes later, they both pulled onto the circular driveway in front of Tranquil Bed and Breakfast. Bryce walked with her to the door, and it swung open right before they reached it.

Erica greeted them with a bright smile. "Megan! Welcome, it's so good to see you." She spoke in a hushed tone, probably so that she didn't disturb the other guests. "Come on in." She ushered them inside. "I heard about the fire. I'm glad you're okay. And I'm sorry to hear about your father."

"Thank you. There's been a lot to process." She accepted a hug. "It's definitely been a crazy night. It's good to see you, too." Megan's gaze swept over the entry and living area. "I'm sorry we woke you up."

"Nonsense. Besides, this is an emergency. I'm sure you're exhausted." Erica glanced at Megan's feet and the purse she carried. "Come on, let's get you set up." She gave Bryce a quick hug, whispering near his ear, "She'll be fine. You're on shift, right? Go back and check in."

He didn't want to leave, but he knew Megan was in good hands. Erica would give her the room she usually held back for emergencies and make sure she had what she needed.

Erica must have sensed his hesitation. "Why don't you come back for breakfast? We're having pancakes, sausage, and eggs. There will be plenty if you want to swing by after you clock out."

Bryce grinned. "You know me too well. Thanks, Erica." He gave Megan a nod. "I hope you can get some rest, and I'll see you in a few hours."

Bryce's mind raced as he pulled away from the B & B.

Later on, he'd check in with Deputy Chief Menendez when he got back to the station and his friend, Arnold Dolman, who was chief at the police department. Maybe they had more information about the fire and whether the arsonist was targeting anyone specific.

"Oh, I can't take these." Megan tried to hand the pajamas—obviously new with tags—back to Erica, but her hostess would have none of it.

"Follow me. Let me show you something." Erica led the way down a dimly lit hallway upstairs to a small room at the end. She turned the light on, illuminating several folding tables piled high with clothing. Shelves lined one wall, each one filled with neatly folded shirts and pairs of jeans. "I help organize the clothing drive for the Church of the Nazarene every year, and this is where we collect everything. Our goal is to make sure people who need clothes—for any reason—have something to wear." Erica gave Megan a firm look. "And losing your luggage in a fire seems like a real need, if you ask me. Especially with the funeral this afternoon." As if to accentuate her point, she motioned to one table containing new packages of socks and underwear. "I insist you take what you need to get you through. Your situation is exactly why we do this. Please."

Megan wanted to object, but how could she when Erica was being so kind? Megan could stop by the store and buy new clothes tomorrow, but she had to have something to wear out in the first place. "I appreciate it, thank you." Besides, she could give a monetary donation to the church to pay for replacement clothing before she left town.

"You're welcome." Erica grinned at her. There was no

doubt she and Bryce were siblings. They shared the same brown hair with blond highlights and piercing blue eyes. Unlike her brother's short-cropped hair, Erica's flowed to the middle of her back. "The bathroom is fully stocked. If you need anything else, please let me know." She pointed to the stairs. "My son and I are downstairs, first door on your right. Breakfast is served at seven, but given everything tonight, I can put a plate aside for you."

"That's okay, I'll set an alarm." She had a whole list of things to do tomorrow and couldn't afford to sleep in. "Thanks again, Erica. And the B & B is beautiful."

Erica gave her one last hug and then made her retreat.

The emotional weight of the day pressed on Megan's shoulders as she chose a pair of jeans, a black blouse, and a light-weight black jacket. At least she'd be appropriately dressed for the funeral. Before heading to her room, she also got new underwear, socks, and some shoes. The fact Erica's church organized something like this was amazing and brought tears to her eyes.

She gathered her things and headed for the bathroom. As she showered, not an easy task when she was trying to keep her bandaged hand dry, thoughts kept swirling in her head. What was it going to be like to see Mom again?

How was she supposed to prepare herself to face the past, when she'd spent years focusing her efforts on forgetting it?

"Fake it till you make it." It'd been one of her mom's favorite sayings when Megan was young.

Apparently, their family had been good at it because no one truly knew what Megan's homelife was like. Her parents were pillars of the community, especially her father. Everyone looked up to him. Respected him.

No one dared question that it might all be a front.

Megan let the stream of water carry the soot away, praying it might ease some of her stress. "Lord, give me strength to deal with today." Her words only echoed in the small space, but a measure of comfort settled over her heart.

Megan turned the water off, stepped out of the shower, and reached for an oversized towel.

Very few people knew the truth about her parents. There was her best friend, Paige Wade, of course. She was the one person Megan had stayed in touch with over the years, and the one bright spot about coming back to Destiny.

And then there was Bryce. He'd suspected things weren't quite right with her family, but they never really talked about it.

Megan's thoughts shifted to her high school boyfriend. Her first love. Breaking things off with him had been one of the most difficult things about leaving Destiny. But she had to put this place behind her. Paige got that. Megan could only pray that Bryce understood, too.

Destiny was his home. He'd always said he wanted to raise a family in the same area near his parents and sister. He deserved someone who wanted the same thing. There was no way Megan could've expected him to choose differently.

Her chest ached, and she rubbed it absently. She'd get through this and drive away from Destiny until the town was nothing but dust in her rearview mirror.

Megan barely stayed awake long enough to get dressed in her new pajamas and climb into bed. As sleep claimed her, the last thing that went through her mind was the look on Bryce's face when he realized who he was rescuing.

Chapter Three

When her phone alarm went off just a few hours later, Megan groaned against the sun peeking around the edge of the curtains. Her eyes ached, and her hand throbbed. She grumbled as she forced herself to sit up and turn her alarm off.

She dragged herself out of bed, dressed quickly, and had just finished getting cleaned up in the bathroom when her cell phone buzzed. Seeing Paige's name on the screen brought a smile to Megan's face. "Hey, Paige," she answered.

"Are you okay? I heard about the fire at your hotel. How horrible!"

"The fire took out a section of the hotel, including my room. But other than a small burn, I'm fine." Megan looked down at her bandaged hand.

"You were hurt? What happened?"

Megan pictured Paige sitting cross legged on her couch, the TV on mute as she watched coverage of the fire. Megan spoke softly and related the night's events to her friend.

"You were actually carried out of the building and

down a ladder by a handsome firefighter?" Paige sounded incredulous.

"I climbed down myself, thank you very much." And yes, the firefighter was handsome. Always had been. But she had no intention of voicing that aloud. "I didn't realize Bryce had become a firefighter."

"Is *he* the one who rescued you?" Paige must have taken Megan's silence as an affirmative. "Oh, wow. We are definitely going to need to revisit that little tidbit of information later." She paused. "So where are you now?"

"I'm staying at the Tranquil Bed and Breakfast." Megan took another look around the room. It was a step up from the hotel.

Paige shuffled something in the background. "I wish you'd come stay at my house."

Megan shook her head even though her friend wouldn't be able to see the motion. "You know how much I appreciate the offer, but you don't have enough room." Paige's tiny two-bedroom apartment was barely big enough to host her parents, who had come from Arizona to visit for a week. "This is fine. Besides, I'll only be here one more night anyway."

"Alright. I know better than to try to change your mind." Paige quieted. "Have you seen your mom yet?"

"Not yet." She hadn't seen either of her parents since she'd left. Sure, she'd spoken to her mom on the phone once a week, but communication both ways had been forced. Contact with her dad had been almost nonexistent.

Megan was too exhausted to dive into the subject. "Are we still on for dinner tonight?"

"Absolutely. I told my parents about you being in town, and they said they could use some downtime while I'm gone." She hesitated. "I ran into Gabe the other day."

"Oh?" Megan thought about their mutual friend. Although she hadn't seen or spoken to him in years, Paige talked about him often enough for Megan to know Gabe Harrison worked for the police department as a K-9 handler.

"I mentioned you were in town, and he commented about how he hoped to run into you. I thought I might invite him to join us for dinner, but only if that sounds good to you, too."

Her friend's hesitation made Megan smile. She'd always suspected some interest between them in high school, and his name still came up in conversation from time to time. "Of course, that would be fun."

"Great!" The excitement had returned to Paige's voice. "I'll text you this afternoon so we can figure out where to eat." She paused again. "I'm sorry I can't be at the funeral. I would if I could—you know that. But I can't wait to see you."

"Like I told you, you don't need to worry about it. And I can't wait, either." It would've been nice to have Paige at the funeral with her. But between her parents being in town and working as one of two vets at a veterinary clinic, Paige had her hands full. "I'll see you tonight, Paige."

"Looking forward to it."

Megan hung up and tried to stifle a yawn, failing miserably. What she really needed was a cup of coffee and something to eat.

It was nearly seven. Bryce would be there soon if he took his sister up on her offer of breakfast.

The moment she opened the door and stepped into the hallway, the scent of maple syrup tangled with tantalizing hints of sausage and drew her downstairs.

A little boy greeted her at the bottom. "Good morning!"

he chirped. "I'll show you where breakfast is!" With that, he took off.

Megan chuckled and followed him to the dining room where a large, farm-style table sat laden with all kinds of food. She counted twelve chairs around it, and four were already occupied by people she didn't recognize.

The little boy brought Erica over. "Here she is, Mama." He looked up at Megan. "Do you like pancakes?"

"Most definitely. How about you?"

He gave her an enthusiastic nod. "I can eat two all by myself!"

Erica shook her head at the boy, a glimmer of love and laughter in her eyes. "This is my son, Peter."

"I'm six years old!"

Erica laughed this time. "Yes, he's six. And very helpful." She gently nudged him toward the table. "Why don't you go take a seat, baby?"

Apparently, he didn't need to be told twice. But before Peter got to the table, he turned a ninety-degree angle to run toward Bryce who'd just entered the room. "Uncle Bryce! Are you here for breakfast? Do you want to sit beside me? Did you see the pretty lady staying with us?"

Bryce ruffled his hair. "Of course, I'm going to sit next to you. And yes, I saw her."

He must have changed out of his uniform before leaving the station. Instead, he wore a pair of jeans and a blue t-shirt that matched the color of his eyes. The fabric stretched across his broad shoulders and accentuated the muscles of his upper arms.

Bryce's gaze slid to Megan. Her pulse sped up, and her cheeks warmed instantly under the soft look in his eyes. She turned her attention to Erica, relieved to have someone else to focus on. "Thanks again for the clothing." She held her arms out to show how the blouse and jacket were a perfect fit. Truthfully, if it weren't for the fact that they might remind her of the funeral, she could see herself wearing the outfit again.

"I'm glad you were able to find something." She glanced at the table. "The Johnsons and Cartwrights said they were getting breakfast out somewhere today, so I think this is everybody. Let's eat, shall we?"

Megan's stomach growled at the thought. The women laughed as they made their way to the table. She found herself sitting between Erica and one of the other guests.

After praying over their meal, Erica motioned for everyone to proceed.

Conversation was light—mostly centered around news of the fire and what the guests had planned for the day. Megan ate way too much of the delicious food and didn't regret a thing. Besides, she didn't know what to expect for the rest of the day, or when she'd eat next. It'd be good to start out with a full belly.

She caught Bryce looking anxiously at his phone several times and then watching her as well. Was he waiting to hear from someone? Maybe his family was expecting him home again soon.

Megan glanced at his left hand and noticed the lack of a wedding ring.

It didn't mean he wasn't married, although she was pretty sure Paige would have let that tidbit slip through in conversation. Not that it really mattered anyway. Once she got through her father's funeral, she'd be escaping Destiny as fast as she could legally drive. Who knew how long it would be before she saw Bryce again?

The thought put a damper on her mood, which was already weighed down by everything she knew she'd be dealing with today. She used a fork to poke what was left of her pancake before setting it down on her plate.

Thankfully, everyone ate relatively quickly and began to disperse, giving Megan the excuse she needed to leave. She planned to swing by the store to replace some of what she'd lost in the fire. After that, she had to stop by the house to see Mom.

The meal she'd enjoyed minutes ago turned into a stone in her stomach as she shouldered her purse, thanked Erica, and stepped onto the porch out front. She hadn't even made it down the steps before the front door opened and closed loudly behind her. Megan was not the least bit surprised to find Bryce behind her.

"Hey," she greeted. "Thanks again for contacting Erica and getting everything set up. I don't know where I would have stayed otherwise."

"You're welcome." He offered her a smile, then nodded to her hand. "How's it feeling?"

"Truthfully? It hurts." A wooden porch swing sat below one of the large oak trees in the front yard. Megan changed course, easing herself onto one side of the swing once they reached it.

Bryce stood in front of her until she motioned for him to take a seat.

The swing shifted from side to side as his weight joined hers. Using the toe of her new-to-her black shoes, Megan gently set the swing in motion. "I've had patients with burns much worse than this. I can only imagine the pain they must have been in."

"I bet it's horrible, especially when they are just kids."

She nodded, mentally blocking some of the images that tried to force their way forward. "The worst cases go to the burn unit. But still ... I hate seeing kids in pain." She paused. "It's being there for them, watching them recover and feel better, that makes it all worth it." Suddenly realizing she probably way overshared, she suddenly lifted her burned hand and flexed the fingers, the motion pulling at the damaged skin of her palm. "Anyway, it'll heal." A quiet chuckle filled her chest. "I'm not sure what surprised me more: flames evicting me from my hotel room or running into you on the ladder."

Bryce's chin lifted as a deep laugh filled the air around him. "If it helps, I was shocked to see you, too."

She studied his profile. In many ways, he was the same Bryce she'd left behind. And yet, he was so very different. More self-assured. Stronger, and it wasn't just the muscles that he'd developed since high school. There was something about having him here that made her feel better. Safer.

Which made sense. He'd chosen to dedicate his life to rescuing others and had saved hers in the process. The man was a hero no matter how you looked at it. It was normal to appreciate and admire that, right?

"So, what about you? What made you decide to pull people out of burning buildings for a living?"

Bryce took over gently tapping the ground with his foot to keep the swing moving. "I never considered it in high school. But a year or so after we graduated, my grandparents survived a house fire. Thanks to the fire department, they not only got out alive, but didn't lose their home." He stared at something in the distance. "I'd spent a lot of my young childhood visiting them and playing in that house. I guess it just hit me then, that those firemen had saved my grandparents in more ways than one. I wanted to be a part of that—to be there for someone during their worst moments. It's why I sometimes volunteer with the search and rescue team, too."

Megan tried to wrap her mind around that. Back in high

school, he'd talked about owning his own business someday. Or possibly going into construction. But working for the fire department? She wouldn't have guessed that for his future in a hundred years. Her thoughts must have been evident on her face because Bryce nudged her shoulder with his.

"Is it so hard to believe I might want to help people?"

"No. Actually, it's not." That was the truth. Somehow, it fit his personality perfectly. "When did Destiny get a search and rescue team?"

"Arnold Dolman is chief of police now. He formed it about six years ago. We've got a solid thirty members who volunteer regularly, though probably only about ten who are hardcore and really get into the training and all that."

"Of which you're one, I'm sure."

He nodded once. There was no air of superiority, just recognizing a simple fact. "My knowledge from working with the fire department has come in handy more than once. We've been called out to help with several things throughout the county."

"I think that's great, Bryce. Good for you."

"Thanks. I'm happy to be a part of it all. But what about you?" He angled his body toward her. "Working with kids—that must be pretty amazing."

"I enjoy it. But there are a lot of politics involving insurance and money that drives me crazy sometimes. I wish we could just help people get better, you know?" It was never that simple. Nothing in life was.

The phone on Bryce's knee jumped to life as the screen lit up. He snatched it and answered the call in one motion. "Keyes here. Any news?" His gaze slid to her face, then focused on the tree line as he listened to the caller on the other end of the phone.

Megan watched as his relaxed expression changed. His

jaw clenched, and a muscle in his neck pulsed. He gave a terse nod as though the person on the other end of the phone might see it. "Roger that. Yep, I'll let you know if I pick up on anything."

With that, Bryce hung up and slowly pocketed his phone. He stood and stepped away from the swing.

"I take it that wasn't good news." It was supposed to be a joke, but when Bryce didn't respond right away, Megan swallowed hard. "And why do I get the feeling it has something to do with me?"

Bryce pivoted to face her and reached for her uninjured hand. Megan might have tried to pull it away if it weren't for the determination in his eyes and the serious timbre in his voice when he said, "The fire last night was set on purpose. It's possible someone tried to kill you."

Chapter Four

Bryce wasn't sure what he expected Megan to do or say, but he certainly didn't anticipate the laughter that followed his announcement.

"You can't be serious." Her hand slipped from his, and she used it to brush some hair back from her cheek.

"The fire started in the hallway immediately outside your hotel room—"

"A careless person probably discarded a cigarette. It happens all the time." The humor in her eyes dimmed some as she watched him warily.

Bryce wished she were right. "They used an accelerant. Megan, the fire was set intentionally. Remember how you couldn't get down the fire escape? It wasn't old or rusted into position. It was recently tied in place along with another half dozen on that same side of the hotel."

Megan's mouth opened as though she wanted to argue and closed again. Finally, she spoke. "This is insane." She tugged at a section of hair and wrinkled her nose. "Wait, you said my fire escape wasn't the only one that was tampered with. Then why are you assuming they're trying to kill me specifically?"

"It's possible someone randomly chose the outside of your room to start the fire, not realizing or caring who was in it." But, until that was proven, there was also a chance Megan was the target. "Look, it was Arnold on the phone, and so far, they've found no connection between the fire and a disgruntled employee or guest at the hotel. At least nothing obvious. They are trying to go through video footage from the security cameras in the hotel now."

"None of this makes any sense." She released a quiet sigh as she sank back against the swing.

Bryce watched as she stared at her hands, the thumb of her uninjured one flicking at the edge of the bandage wrapped around the other.

She must have come to a decision because she straightened again and leaned forward until her feet were firmly planted on the ground. "Then I'll make sure Mom's okay, go to the funeral, and hopefully, head back to San Antonio tomorrow."

Bryce held up a hand to stop her. "Whoa, if someone wanted you dead, who's to say they won't try again?"

"That's just it. We can't know if I was even the target, much less what else this insane person has planned. If anything at all." Megan stood. The swing swayed unevenly behind her. "Which means there's no reason why I shouldn't tie things up here. I won't even need a full twenty-four hours."

Of course she planned to leave Destiny as soon as she could. The fact she hadn't visited once since she left should prove she didn't think there was anything worth staying for. Why would she stick around after the funeral?

Bryce knew all this, but somehow hearing her announce

her plans aloud hit him harder than it should have. Like an idiot, he'd hoped she might have been even half as curious about him as he was about her. It shouldn't bother him—anything between them ended long ago—but it did.

He shoved his disappointment into the closet of his mind where it belonged. "You want to get out of town as fast as you can. I get it, Megan. But until you do, you could be in danger."

Megan groaned. "What do you want me to do about it?"

Bryce wished he had some answers for her. Instead, he slipped his hands into the pockets of his jeans and simply said, "You can let me go with you today. Just to keep watch so you don't have to worry about it."

Her eyes widened at his suggestion. "I think you're overreacting."

"I don't."

She immediately shook her head. "It's completely unnecessary. I'm sure you have something more important to do today."

"I just started my forty-eight off. Please, Megan. I won't bother you. Let me escort you today and see if anyone is hanging around. If we're overreacting, then there's no harm done. But if someone is targeting you..." Bryce prayed she'd see his point. Truthfully, he was planning to shadow her anyway, and it'd be a whole lot easier if he had her permission. "Well, let's just say having someone else watching your back isn't a bad idea."

Megan's eyes slid shut for several moments before they snapped open again and her gaze zeroed in on him. "Fine. On one condition." She pointed a finger at him. "We keep all of this on the downlow. We don't need to freak people out for no reason, especially my mom."

Bryce held a hand up in surrender. "I couldn't agree

with you more." Relief flooded his system knowing he would be able to keep an eye on her. "So where are we off to first?"

Megan frowned. "I have to stop at the store and buy some clothing." She motioned to the outfit she'd gotten from Erica. "That way I'll have something to change into after the funeral. Then I need to go by Mom's house."

There was no missing the resolute tone of her voice. As far as Bryce knew, her parents still lived in the same home they'd owned when she left. He imagined going back would be a weird experience after so long. He had all kinds of questions, but he limited it to one. "Do you want to take your car or my truck? I'm happy to drive either way, and you can give your hand a rest."

"I'd prefer my car. And if you want to drive, that would be great." The burn must be hurting more than she let on for her to relinquish control so quickly.

He nodded his agreement and motioned for her to lead the way to her car. As soon as they got inside, her phone rang. She answered it and spoke to someone for several minutes as he made their way across to the northeast side of town.

When she hung up, she said, "That was Paige. I left her a message early this morning, but she wanted to make sure I was okay."

"I'm glad the two of you kept in touch." The girls had been close back in the day, and he'd envied Paige that connection since then. It'd taken everything in him to not regularly ask how Megan was. At least Paige had taken pity on him in the beginning and let him know Megan was okay, even if she never revealed where her best friend had moved to.

Bryce pulled into the parking lot at the local Walmart.

He stayed nearby but gave her space to shop and check out. Back at the car, he took the bags from her and stored them in the trunk.

Ten minutes later, they'd driven across Destiny and were nearing her parents' house. It was one of the more affluent parts of town, and one that her family, given her father's successful car dealership, seemed to fit right in with.

Bryce turned left onto Magnolia Avenue and slowed the car as they approached the large, two-story home that Bryce remembered well. He'd picked Megan up at that black front door more times than he could count. Kissed her good night there, too.

He glanced at her profile as she stared at the house, a mix of emotions marching across her face. What was she remembering right now? He was sure heated kisses beneath the porch light were probably way down on the list.

Bryce bit back a sigh of frustration—as much toward himself as anything—for allowing himself to go down memory lane when he ought to steer clear of it.

Megan captured her bottom lip between her teeth and slowly released her seat belt.

He looked up and down the street but didn't see anything or anyone out of the ordinary. "You ready for this?"

"Not even a little."

Megan truly hoped to never set foot in her childhood home again. Seeing the large house stirred up dread along with a generous helping of panic. Even knowing her father wouldn't be inside did little to help.

Echoes of her father yelling, and the sting of his anger

against her skin, threatened to overwhelm Megan. She'd never be able to forget the heavy weight of uselessness she'd felt while watching her mom cower in fear.

No, there were few warm feelings associated with the place, and any she could conjure had more to do with Bryce than her parents.

She glanced at the man sitting in the driver's seat of her car. How many times had he brought her home after school or a date? Way more times than she could count. Now Bryce watched her, compassion coming off him in waves.

Megan didn't want his pity. Just like she hadn't wanted it back in high school. But as much as she hated to admit it, having Bryce with her took the edge off her nerves.

If nothing else, maybe his presence would serve as a buffer when it came to Mom. It'd worked when they were teens, anyway. After all, neither of her parents wanted Bryce or anyone else to see anything but a picture of the perfect family. Having him with her had made Megan feel safe. She tried not to analyze the way it all came flooding back now.

Determined to get this over with, Megan got out of the car and squared her shoulders. At the door, she lifted the knocker and let it fall against the metal plate behind it. She wasn't sure Mom was going to answer at first, but then the sound of a lock sliding out of place preceded the turn of the doorknob.

When the door opened, Megan couldn't believe the older woman looking through the opening was her mother. The last nine years, coupled with her husband's death, hadn't necessarily been kind to her.

The moment Mom saw her, her chin quivered. "Oh, Megan. It's you, sweetie."

Megan braced herself as Mom engulfed her in a hug, an

overwhelming floral scent surrounding them. Megan awkwardly patted her back. "Yeah, Mom. I'm here. I'm so sorry." And she was. Sorry for Mom's loss. For what she'd been through. "Are you okay?"

Mom nodded. "I still can't believe your father is gone." Her voice caught. She pulled Megan in again. "I'm so glad you came home. I wasn't sure that you would." The words tumbled out between sobs.

Guilt stabbed at Megan's heart, and she bristled at the word "home" and the way Mom used it. Had she wanted to come back to Destiny? No. But this was different. No matter how she felt about her father, she wasn't going to let Mom go to the funeral alone. She also knew her mom and that boundaries were critical with her. "I'm just here to check on you and go to the funeral, Mom. I'm heading out again tomorrow."

Mom rocked her back and forth for a few moments before gently pushing Megan away from her, tears glistening on her cheeks but all sobs on hold. "Is that all? But I need your help with so many things."

As if Mom only just noticed Megan wasn't alone, her attention shifted. "Bryce Keyes? What are you doing here?" She looked at Megan. "Are the two of you back together again?"

"No."

"No, ma'am."

Their well-timed responses had Mom frowning. "Well, that's too bad. I always thought you'd either get my daughter knocked up or marry her. Either way, at least she would've stayed in town." With that comment, she ushered them into the house and closed the door behind them.

And there it is.

Wendy Bristow was a force of nature.

Oh, Megan had heard all about the many mistakes she made in moving away. To hear those conversations boiled down to such a blunt statement caused heat to flood her cheeks. Megan dipped her chin, hoping her hair would hide the blush from Bryce.

It was amazing how quickly Mom was able to turn off the waterworks. She was good at manipulating people with her emotions while Dad used his money and political skills to do the same thing. Megan tried to ignore the familiar tendrils of resentment.

Mom led the way to the large living room. "Can I get you something?"

"Mom, why don't you sit down, and I'll get us all some coffee?" It looked like she was going to protest but gently eased herself into one of the recliners. A surge of worry went through Megan. No matter how strong Mom tried to be, it was clear she was struggling. Megan tried to imagine Mom on her own, caring for herself without her husband hovering in the background, and couldn't.

As Megan walked away from the living room, she could hear Mom and Bryce conversing and tried not to worry about what they were talking about.

When she had coffee ready, she added everything to a tray. She found a package of cookies in the pantry and carried that back to the living room, too.

She sat in the other recliner and glanced across the coffee table at Bryce on the couch. He'd quickly claimed two of the cookies.

Mom caught sight of the cream and sugar on the tray and scowled. "We should drink it black today. That's the way your father liked it, and I think it'd be nice to drink it in his honor."

Megan took the mug Mom offered and cradled it for

several moments before setting it down on the coffee table. She wasn't drinking it black, and certainly not in her father's honor. She was relieved when Bryce set his own mug beside hers without drinking any of the liquid, even if he tossed her a curious look.

Mom didn't seem to notice. She took a sip of the coffee herself and made a face. She'd always taken her coffee one way: with more sugar than actual coffee. But then, when it came to her husband, Mom always made her decisions according to what he wanted. She leaned back with a sigh. "I'm glad you're here, Megan. I need your help to find your father's will and the deed to the dealership."

Megan blinked at her. "What? A lawyer or the bank doesn't have a copy of those?"

Mom shook her head. "You know your father; he didn't trust the bank." She paused and blinked several times. "He liked to keep everything close by, so he knew exactly where it was."

He was controlling. Except Megan didn't say it out loud. "I'm sure you can get copies of them somewhere. Maybe you could try calling around on Monday?"

"No." Mom set her coffee cup on the table with a clunk. "Your father took a second mortgage out on the house. If I can't find a way to pay the balance..." She covered her mouth with one hand as though trying to decide how much to say. "I found a foreclosure notice on your father's desk the other day. I finally went to look at it this morning." She shook her head sadly. "I had no idea, Megan. But I can't lose this house—not after I've already lost your father." Fresh tears raced each other down Mom's cheeks.

Megan knelt beside the chair, offering her mom a comforting hug. "There has to be an explanation. Dad loved this place. He wouldn't have put it in jeopardy like that."

Mom dabbed at her eyes with a small napkin. "I need to find where he keeps all his paperwork, so we can get this figured out." She blinked at Megan. "Will you help me?"

"Of course I will." Because what else could she say? She certainly couldn't leave if her mom was on the verge of being homeless. Though Megan suspected Mom was exaggerating. "Have you gone through his office?"

"I started, but there's so much in there. I got overwhelmed." Mom sniffed and blew her nose. "Will you look, Megan? See if you can find the paperwork?" She watched Megan expectantly.

"Right now?" But when Mom just kept looking at her, Megan knew she had little choice.

"I could lose everything. You could lose your inheritance."

Megan strangled the objection forming in her throat. It didn't matter what her father left behind. She wanted nothing to do with it. But telling Mom that now would only upset her.

"Sure, if that's what you need me to do. Why don't you go and get some rest? Do you need me to do anything around the house for you?"

"No. My housekeeper was by yesterday."

"Okay." Megan would have happily helped with anything else if it delayed a visit to her father's office. She glanced at Bryce who had stood and clearly intended to go with her. "If you need me, just call."

Relief lit up Mom's features. "Thank you. I knew I could count on you." She picked up her coffee cup and stared at the dark liquid inside.

Megan motioned for Bryce to follow her upstairs to her father's office. As they approached the door, Megan stalled.

She was never allowed inside this room. Dad made sure

she knew there were consequences if she stepped a toenail inside, and Megan never forgot it. She crossed her arms in front of her at the memory, then hissed when pressure against her forgotten injured hand resulted in radiating pain.

A warm hand cupped her shoulder. Megan turned to find Bryce standing behind her, his chest mere inches from her back. "Are you okay?" he whispered.

Megan shook her head. His hand slid to the small of her back, and she focused on the pressure as they stepped into the office together.

The normally pristine room was a mess. Several file folders were strewn about the desk, file cabinets pulled open, and even the closet doors left wide, something her father never would've allowed. Everything always had its place.

Megan swiveled to look at Bryce. "Why on earth would my dad take a second mortgage out on this house? As far as I know, they owned it free and clear. That seems like an unusually risky thing to do." She picked up a folder and looked at it before dropping it again.

"Maybe the dealership was struggling," Bryce suggested. He let his hand fall from her back and shifted to face her. "You don't look at all comfortable here."

Megan lowered her voice. "I've only been in this office one time."

"Ever?" The surprise was evident in Bryce's voice.

Megan nodded. The memory of that day swam to the surface, and she cringed. "Dad forbade me from ever going into his office. But he had a Newton's cradle—" She pointed to the device still situated on a back corner of the mahogany desk. "I was seven, and it kept calling to me. I wanted to know how it worked. I snuck in here and pulled that first ball back and watched it hit the others." She still recalled the few moments of joy she'd experienced before her father's shadow fell across the desk.

"He caught you, didn't he?"

"Yeah." She paused for a moment, unsure whether she should continue the story or not. But she'd already started it, and Bryce was watching her expectantly. "He got a belt out of the closet, used it on me enough times that I lost count of the swats, and said he didn't want to see me until the next day. I spent the rest of the afternoon and evening in my room."

The muscles in Bryce's jaw tightened. "Did they at least bring dinner up to you?"

"No. I didn't eat until breakfast the next morning." She shrugged, as though it weren't a big deal. Skipping meals happened frequently enough back then—it was one of her father's favorite punishments.

But it was a big deal, and the stricken look on Bryce's face confirmed it.

"Why didn't you tell me about that while we were dating?"

"Because I didn't want you to feel sorry for me." Her gaze narrowed as she stared at him, daring him to disagree and say he would have felt any other way.

He looked like he wanted to argue. "I had no idea, Megan. I'm sorry."

She shrugged again. "It was what it was." She let her gaze fall on the Newton's cradle. What once held her fascination had quickly become a reminder of the control her dad had over her, and the consequences of trying to defy him.

A sick curiosity drew her to the closet. She looked inside, but there was no sign of the belt that he used to keep there. He'd assured her it was always present, waiting for her to sneak back in. Had he been lying throughout her childhood, or had he moved it after she'd left Destiny? Megan supposed she might never know. "I don't understand why Mom stayed with him."

Bryce gave her a sympathetic look. "Do you want some help searching?"

He was clearly offering a change in conversation, and she was happy to accept. She scanned the office. Between the three drawers in the desk, two large filing cabinets, and whatever might be in the closet, it was like looking for a needle in a haystack. "You still have time to escape if you make a run for it now." She was only partially kidding.

He laughed at that. "You're stuck with me."

"Then yes, please." The office smelled like tobacco and suddenly left Megan feeling as though the walls were closing in as the air thickened. Even though her jacket was light, it was still too much. Megan slipped it off and draped it over the arm of her father's chair. She turned to hear Bryce growl, a look of alarm passing over his features.

Chapter Five

Bryce noticed an ugly bruise on Megan's upper arm the moment she took her jacket off. It was dark purple, the outer edges turning a sickly shade of yellow-green. But what alarmed him the most was that it was clearly caused by a human hand—and a large one at that.

Megan appeared confused until she realized what he was looking at. Instinctively, she reached for her jacket again. "It looks worse than it feels."

"I sure hope so." He strode forward and gingerly took the jacket from her and placed it back on the chair so he could get a better look at the bruise. To leave one like that, somebody had to have grabbed her arm and jerked her around. Hard. The idea that anyone would cause her harm like that had his blood boiling. "Who did this to you? If someone is hurting you..."

"It's nothing like that." She stepped away from him, her voice calm. "We had a patient come in complaining of intense pain. Turns out he was an addict that was hoping to get a prescription for Vicodin. We discharged him, but he became angry and tried to coerce me into giving him access to the medicine cabinet. This bruise and a small cut—" she shifted hair over to show a scab near the top of her left ear— "were the results. It's just part of the job."

Bryce wanted to argue, but she was right. He understood that as well as anyone. He was often at risk of injury whenever he responded to a fire. And if something happened, while it would be horrible, he'd signed up for it.

That didn't mean he liked the image of a drug addict threatening Megan, though. "Do you know if the man was arrested?"

"I'm assuming so. Hospital security took him into custody." Megan turned her head slightly and studied his face. "Why? What are you thinking?"

It was just a hunch, but with little evidence pointing to who might be behind the possible attack on Megan, Bryce was willing to run with anything right now. "I'm wondering if he might have followed you here. Maybe he's angry enough to try and pay you back for not only refusing to give him the medication, but getting him arrested, too."

"That seems pretty far-fetched." She paused, clearly mulling the idea over. "I mean, assuming someone really had targeted me, why would he follow me here instead of trying to get to me back in San Antonio?"

All good questions. But it was too strong of a coincidence to ignore. "I'll call over and talk to Arnold anyway. At least he should be able to check and see if the guy's still locked up or not." He got the name of the hospital she worked at and the day of the incident and made a note of them on his phone.

That seemed to satisfy her. She nodded before releasing

a heavy sigh as she looked around the room. "I guess we'd better get busy. And I'll bet you're already sorry you offered to shadow me today."

He smiled at her. "Not at all." Did she regret agreeing to it? He hoped not.

"In that case, pick a drawer, any drawer," she said, motioning to the desk.

Bryce called Arnold and told him about the man who assaulted Megan in San Antonio. Arnold said he'd check into it and let Bryce know what he found.

After that, they sifted through papers for nearly two hours and never heard a peep from Mrs. Bristow. Bryce wondered several times if they should check on her. He looked up from the stack of papers he was going through and noticed Megan with her back to a wall and her forehead resting against the palm of her left hand. "Hey." He sat on the floor beside her. When she didn't look up, he lightly touched her knee. "A lot has happened in the last two days. It's okay to give yourself time to process."

She shook her head. When she finally looked up, determination filled her features. "I hate this. All of it. Seeing Mom upset. Digging around in my dad's office." She paused. "Normally, this should make me feel sad. But it doesn't. Not even a little." Her shoulders slumped. "What kind of person does that make me?" She didn't give him time to answer. "And then here you are. You shouldn't have been dragged into this. Of all the people in town who should hate me—who shouldn't want to see me—it's you."

"Megan. You have no idea how upset I was when you left. I was angry. Hurt. I thought what we had between us meant more to you than that. But..." When she ducked her chin, he put a finger under it and gently lifted her eyes to

44

his. "But I've had nine years to think about it. To move forward. To realize I couldn't possibly understand. Life has happened, Megan. To both of us. Picking at the past isn't going to do either of us any good."

He mostly meant what he said. The truth was, seeing her again had reawakened the attraction he'd always had toward her. But it'd also brought back the pain when she'd left him behind. The combination was more than a little confusing.

Her hazel eyes stayed focused on his face for several heartbeats, disbelief mixed with the pain swirling in their depths. "I really want a glass of whatever Kool Aid you've been drinking."

Bryce laughed then. A loud, boisterous laugh that had Megan joining in. It was the kind of laugh born of necessity, allowing the tension to ease a little.

Megan swiped at the corner of her eyes. "I needed that." She released a long sigh. "For what it's worth, I've missed you, Bryce."

"I've missed you, too. You know, for what it's worth." He reached over and fiddled with the latch on the file cabinet nearby.

There was so much more Bryce could've said. Questions he wanted to ask. Things about the last nine years that he should probably tell her about, including the fact that he'd been engaged at one point. But this didn't seem like the time. They got back to looking through stacks and stacks of papers.

Why hadn't she felt like she could talk to him back in the day? She'd alluded to not getting along with her father, but she'd never cued Bryce in on what sounded like abusive behavior toward her. Did her mother know?

Bryce subtly studied Megan, admiring the way her hair curved slightly at her chin. Having her here now was more like an echo of the past, and he'd do well to remember it. He'd be a fool to want to get to know her again. Especially when she was in such a hurry to leave town.

He focused on searching through paperwork. Unfortunately, they were no closer to finding the will or deed than when they first started.

An hour before the funeral, Mrs. Bristow came rushing into the room wearing a fancy black dress with shoes and a bag to match. Her gray hair was pulled back into some kind of updo that definitely added to the impression of wealth that she exuded. "Did you find them?" The hope in her eyes immediately faded when Megan got to her feet and shook her head.

"Sorry, Mom. We didn't find either document. Maybe they aren't here. Did you guys have a safe deposit box at the bank or anything like that?"

"I ... don't know." Mrs. Bristow looked lost as she stared unseeing through the large office window. With a start, she focused on her daughter again. "We'll need to leave soon. I'd like to see my Richard before everyone starts to arrive, and I'm sure you would as well." With that, she left the office, her back straight and her heels clicking down the stairs to the first floor.

Megan turned woodenly to follow her mom.

Bryce resisted the urge to put an arm around her and pull her close. The last thing he wanted to do was make things more uncomfortable for either of them. Still, he wished things were easier for her somehow.

46

The entire viewing, funeral, and graveside service passed like a blur for Megan. It was surreal to see so many people come in support of her father while singing his praises. They kept approaching Megan, too, telling her how they were glad she was back, and how wonderful it was for her to be there for Mom.

The first dozen times, she tried to come up with a response. But after that, she embraced the role of a grief-stricken daughter and only nodded her acknowledgment. That was okay, right? After all, wasn't that the part she was supposed to play?

Through it all, Bryce was by her side. Somehow, he instinctively seemed to know how close to stay to be supportive without smothering her. Not only that, but he was constantly on alert. She didn't really put much stock in the idea that someone was out to kill her, but knowing he was aware of everything going on didn't hurt.

After the graveside service, they had the reception at a church a block down from the funeral home. Megan wasn't sure of the connection between Mom and the church, but they set up a lovely late lunch complete with sandwiches, salads, and desserts.

A large picture of her father propped on a wooden easel greeted Megan when she entered. His mouth was stretched in a smile she'd only ever seen reserved for public appearances. She fought a flinch and hurried past. Mom seemed to soak in the attention and love shown by members of the community.

Megan quickly found a corner of the room near a large, artificial palm tree and didn't hesitate to pull a folding chair over there. Thankfully no one—including Mom—noticed her.

Well, almost no one.

Bryce walked up, a plate laden with a variety of sandwiches in one hand and two cans of soda balanced in the other. He handed the icy cans to Megan before bringing another chair over to join her. He retrieved a Dr Pepper from her, then held the plate out.

Megan didn't feel like eating, but she took a small ham and cheese sandwich anyway. "Thank you." Now the Coke, she could use that for sure. Caffeine? Yes, please. She popped it open and took a long swig.

"You're welcome." He took a drink of his own soda before finishing one of the small sandwiches in two bites. He tapped her shoe with his. "How many people here do you actually know?"

She surveyed the large room and counted silently. "Maybe ten." She finished her sandwich, then gently pressed her cold can of soda against her injured palm and winced. Too bad she hadn't brought some acetaminophen with her. The long drive back tomorrow was going to stink. Just thinking about gripping the steering wheel made her hand ache. "It just goes to show how little we can really know about the people we spend our time with."

Bryce popped a second sandwich in his mouth. When he'd swallowed, he shot her a curious look. "Are you referring to yourself, your mom, or the guests?"

"Maybe all the above. But mostly the guests. If they'd really known my father..." her voice faltered. "Let's just say my family was an expert on putting up a big front."

"You never did." He spoke without hesitation. "At least it never seemed that way."

"There were things I didn't tell you back then. Not because I was trying to keep secrets, but because I was living through it all at the time. When I finally got away from the house, I wanted to pretend things were normal, you know?"

"I can understand that. I may not have known what was going on, but I could tell there was a lot of strain in your family." He balanced the plate on the top of the palm tree planter. "I never asked you about it, though. I should have. That's on me."

Megan immediately shook her head, hating that he felt guilty about the past. "There's no guarantee I would've wanted to talk about it even if you had asked. We were both young. Dumb. It was what it was." She had plenty of her own regrets and guilt surrounding her senior year of high school. Most of them had something to do with Bryce. "The fact I left so I didn't have to deal with it all should tell you that."

"Maybe. But I wish I could've been the kind of man— the kind of friend—you felt comfortable talking to." His words were low but sincere.

They brought tears to her eyes. "I'm sorry, Bryce. You deserved to be treated better. If it helps, I hated myself for leaving you like I did." She doubted an apology, many years too late, meant much to him. To her surprise, he reached for her uninjured hand and gave it a firm squeeze before releasing it again when his cell phone rang.

She took another drink and listened as he answered the call.

"Hey, Arnold. What have you got?" He paused as he listened, lines forming between his brows. He frowned. "Any idea where he might be now? Okay." Another pause as he glanced at Megan. "She still insists she's driving home first thing tomorrow. I'll let you know if anything changes." He ended the call before slipping the phone into his pocket. "Arnold checked into the man who attacked you at the hospital. His name is Wallace McBride. A family member posted bail within forty-eight hours. We aren't sure where he is right now, but Arnold has his people looking into it."

"It seems crazy the guy would follow me all the way here. Why wait? Why not go after me in San Antonio last week instead?" Megan swallowed hard. Truthfully, she'd worried about him showing up at the hospital again, but he never had.

"I'm sure you're right. But since we have no other leads at this point, we need to rule him out as a suspect." He finished his can of soda. "You've hardly eaten anything. Can I get you another sandwich?"

"No, thank you. I'm meeting Paige and Gabe for dinner tonight." There was no containing the excitement in her voice. Back in high school, the four of them did a lot together. Suddenly, the idea of eating dinner with them, and not including Bryce, seemed wrong. "You're free to join us if you want to." The words spilled out of her mouth before she'd thought it through.

Then again, she may as well invite him. He'd probably be tailing her anyway if she didn't. She hadn't missed the way he frequently scanned the room and kept an eye on all the doors leading in and out. Besides, Bryce and Gabe used to be good friends. It wasn't all that weird for Megan to invite him along, and she knew Paige wouldn't mind.

Bryce looked surprised but quickly agreed. "Sure. That sounds like fun."

Someone approached them, and Megan looked up to see an older woman, maybe ten years younger than Mom. She glanced over her shoulder before positioning herself so that her back was to the rest of the people in the reception hall. "My name is Helen Gadd. I work as a receptionist at your father's dealership. I wanted to talk to you about some-thing while Wendy wasn't around."

Megan thought the woman seemed nervous. "Is every-thing okay?"

Helen hesitated for a fraction of a second before responding. "It's about your mom." She lowered her voice. "Look, she needs your help."

Chapter Six

Helen's insistent voice had Bryce leaning forward in his seat. He quickly sought out Mrs. Bristow, relieved to see she seemed well and safe amidst her friends across the room.

Megan looked doubtful. "What makes you say that?"

"Before your father died, there was a lot of discussion between him and Gary—your father's manager. I never could hear what they were talking about, but the conversations often became heated, and neither of them seemed happy." Helen looked conflicted. "I heard your father was behind on payments to the bank. I just know your mother seems confused, and I'm afraid someone is going to take advantage of her. I got the impression your father handled everything when it came to finances."

That idea didn't seem to surprise Megan. "And you want me to talk to my mom?"

Helen nodded enthusiastically, her short, curly hair bouncing. "Maybe make some inquiries." Her eyes teared up, and her voice caught. "I don't want someone to take advantage of her."

Bryce watched Megan as doubt flitted across her face quickly followed by concern and finally a hint of defeat. She leaned against the back of her chair.

Megan forced a smile. "I appreciate you letting me know. I'll look into it."

Helen nodded once and hurried away.

Megan looked at Bryce and sighed. "What are the odds the dealership and the bank are open on Sunday?"

He frowned. She'd been counting down the hours until she could leave town. Now, if she wanted to follow up on any of this, she'd have to delay her escape until Monday at the earliest. It was only an extra day, but it was clearly asking for a lot. "The dealership might be."

She nodded as though that offered at least a little hope.

They sat in silence for another half hour. Finally, the gathering began to break up, and soon, Mrs. Bristow was telling the last person goodbye. When she was done, she let out a long sigh. "I guess that's it."

The poor woman, she looked utterly lost.

"Why don't we follow you back to your house? Make sure you get there okay."

Megan shot him a surprised look. He probably should've checked with her first. But honestly, he would've offered whether Megan was there or not.

Mrs. Bristow nodded. "I appreciate that."

Members of the church helped place several large flower arrangements in Mrs. Bristow's car before they headed back to her house. She parked in the driveway, and Bryce parked on the street out front.

He got out of the car and was going to offer to carry the flower arrangements inside when the front of the house snagged his attention. The door caught a breeze and slowly opened before shutting again.

"Mrs. Bristow? Was someone watching the house for you during the funeral?"

The older woman looked confused until she saw the door. Her frown and the alarm on her face told him she hadn't expected anyone to come by. "No. No one."

Bryce motioned to Megan. "Stay with her." He took out his phone and dialed Arnold. "Hey. I'm at Mrs. Bristow's place, and it looks like someone broke in." He gave the address and then stepped close enough to get a better look at the door. "Definitely signs of forced entry."

"I'm sending someone your way. Can you tell if anyone is still inside?"

"I can't. But the front door is wide open, so I'm guessing whoever broke in is long gone."

"An officer should be at your location in five."

"Understood." Bryce put his phone away and rejoined Megan and her mom where they waited until Gabe Harrison's Tahoe arrived, the words "K-9 Unit" on the side.

Gabe approached them with his German shepherd, Loki, on a leash at his side. He gave Megan a nod in greeting. Another police car pulled up behind Gabe's vehicle, and an officer got out. "Please stay out here. We're going to go clear the house." He and the other officer approached the house. Gabe withdrew his service weapon, issued Loki a command, and the trio quietly entered the building.

When they came back out, Gabe had already returned his weapon to his holster, then jogged over to them. He stopped, and Loki sat beside him. "Mrs. Bristow, I'm sorry to say that someone did break into your home. It looks like they used a crowbar to get inside. The good news is that most of your home looks untouched. Whoever did this focused their efforts on the office and master bedroom." Another police car pulled up. "They'll dust the place for prints, take pictures and then probably have you go through to see if anything is missing." He glanced at the house, hoping to see evidence of a doorbell camera or something similar. "Do you have a security system?"

Mrs. Bristow shook her head. "Richard hated the very idea of it. He insisted that people could hack into it and use it to spy on us instead." She wrung her hands together, then lifted her head as someone caught her attention. "Oh! Vincent!" She stepped away from them and onto the sidewalk where she flagged down a mail carrier.

The middle-aged man looked up from the mail he was holding and frowned when he saw the commotion. "Are you okay, Mrs. Bristow?"

"Someone broke into my home. I don't suppose you saw anything, did you?"

"No, ma'am. I wish I had." Vincent's brows pinched together. "Some people just have no shame, do they? No shame."

One of the new officers approached. "Do you usually deliver mail to this neighborhood?"

Bryce left them to talk and swallowed his disappointment. Still, maybe a neighbor's camera caught the criminal. He'd mention the possibility to Gabe, although his friend was probably already two steps ahead.

Mrs. Bristow, who suddenly seemed older, moved to sit back in the driver's seat of her vehicle. "I can't believe this is happening. Today of all days."

Megan patted her shoulder awkwardly before walking several steps away from the car.

Gabe was waiting for her when she turned back around, a smile on his face. "I was hoping to run into you, though I'm sorry it was under these circumstances." He stepped forward and pulled her into a brief hug. "It's good to see you, Megan."

"You, too." She motioned to Loki. "I'd heard you were part of a K-9 unit. Looks like it fits you well."

"That it does." He rested a hand on Loki's head and gave it a pat. "Paige mentioned dinner tonight. I'm looking forward to it." He turned to look at Bryce. "You ought to join us," he offered as they shook hands.

Bryce spoke to Gabe on a regular basis but couldn't remember the last time they'd done something as friends. "Megan invited me, and I wouldn't miss it."

"Great! It's like getting the whole gang back together again, isn't it?" He glanced in the direction of the house. "Look, I should go see if there's anything we can do to help. I'll come back when I have an update." With a last wave, he and Loki jogged away.

Together, Bryce and Megan watched as several officers conversed near the front door of the house.

She turned to him and spoke low. "Whoever did this must have known my mother was going to be at the funeral."

"My thoughts exactly. Unfortunately, something like this isn't uncommon. The church I attend will even send someone to housesit during a funeral to make sure no one bothers it."

Megan's jaw dropped. "I had no idea." She shook her head sadly. "That's seriously messed up."

"Yeah, it is." He didn't know where Mr. and Mrs. Bristow kept their valuables, but hopefully they'd been well hidden. It was bad enough the poor woman had to bury her husband today, and now she had to deal with this. He remembered seeing a guest book when they first got to the reception. "We'll have to see if we can get a list of the people who attended the funeral. I'm sure the police will want something to compare names to. Although it could've been anyone who saw the obituary in the paper."

The next hour started off waiting for the police to finish gathering evidence and ended with Megan and Mrs. Bristow doing a walkthrough of the house to see if anything was missing. Some items were damaged in both the master bedroom and the office, but nothing obvious had been taken.

Mrs. Bristow stood staring at the bedroom, her hands worrying the handle of her purse.

Gabe caught Bryce's attention and motioned him over. Megan joined them. Gabe glanced at Mrs. Bristow in the other room and lowered his voice. "Nothing valuable is missing, including the big screen TV, items from the jewelry box in the bedroom, or the relatively expensive paintings hung throughout the house." He reached down and rested a hand on his dog's head. "It doesn't feel like a typical break-in to me. I'd say that someone may have spooked the intruder, except there was significant ransacking both in the bedroom and the office."

"Whoever did this was looking for something specific." Bryce couldn't ignore the way the hair stood up on the back of his neck.

"But what were they looking for?" asked Megan.

"And did they find it?" The last question came from Gabe. "We're going to canvas the area, ask around in case someone might have seen the intruder go in or come out. Meanwhile, I suggest Mrs. Bristow find somewhere else to stay."

As though she'd been summoned, Mrs. Bristow stepped through the doorway into the hall. "I most certainly will not." Her eyes teared up. "I haven't been sleeping in there anyway. Not without my Richard. I've been staying in the spare room down the hall."

It was clear she'd made up her mind. Gabe gave a short nod. "Then I'll make some calls and see how quickly we can get that front door replaced." With that, he stepped away.

Mrs. Bristow turned to her daughter, a sad look on her face. "Are you still planning to go home tomorrow?"

Now that was the question of the hour. Bryce watched Megan as she thought through her response.

"I'll need to call my boss first, but I'll see if I can stay through Monday. Maybe I can help you find the will and deed after all."

Mrs. Bristow gave her daughter a hug. "I'm so glad. You know, I have plenty of room here ..."

"I know, Mom. But I have a room at the B & B. I'm just going to stay there. But I'd feel better if you came with me. Or spent the night with a friend."

"Nonsense. I have no intention of staying anywhere but here." She waved her hand at the many people coming in and out of rooms. "Besides, after seeing all of these officers, no one is going to come back."

Bryce had a feeling Arnold would increase patrols in the area for the next couple of days, too. But Megan looked uncertain. Mrs. Bristow, on the other hand, seemed happy with her decision and moved toward the office. "Do you think your boss will give you the time off?"

"We're pretty shorthanded in the peds ward right now. But Janet is a good friend. She's also checking in on my cat while I'm gone. If I tell her the situation, she'll encourage me to stay longer."

"You own a cat?" He tried to picture her with one and failed.

Megan grinned. "His name is Smokey. He's a gray

tabby. Real original, I know." She shrugged. "Anyway, I'm pretty sure he'd argue with you over who owns who."

Bryce laughed at that. "Sounds about right for a cat." He watched as Mrs. Bristow left the office and went farther down the hall looking a little lost. "I feel so bad for your mom."

Megan's gaze followed his. She pursed her lips together for several moments before saying, "She's too stubborn. If it were me, I'd be nervous to stay here alone." She sighed. "Mom's looking for paperwork, Helen says she needs help, and then this happens. What are the odds it's all a coincidence?"

Not to mention the fire at the hotel. He didn't say that aloud, but based on her expression, he was pretty sure it'd crossed her mind, too. "I don't know. But an awful lot has happened in a short period of time. If there's not a connection somewhere..."

"...then it's got to be some epic string of bad luck."

Chapter Seven

Megan basked in the sound of Paige, Gabe, and Bryce laughing. They'd decided to eat at a pizza place in town. While it might be a newer business, it echoed with nostalgia. Between the smell of fresh crust and the sounds of games coming from the arcade room, it was a blast from Megan's past.

How many times had she and her friends scarfed pizza on a Friday night, challenged each other to arcade games, and talked for hours?

They were in their late twenties now, more mature, or so Megan would like to think. But something about being here with them wrapped her in a comforting familiarity she hadn't realized she'd been missing.

For the first time since she got back, she experienced a pang of sadness at the thought of leaving again. No, it didn't overshadow the need to escape as soon as possible, but it was there, and she hadn't seen it coming.

She watched, a smile on her face, as Gabe and Bryce argued back and forth about the last time the four of them had hung out together.

"It was after prom," Bryce insisted.

Gabe looked doubtful for a moment, and then his face lit up. He and Bryce pointed to each as they spoke simultaneously, "Senior prank."

Megan laughed as she remembered how most of the senior class had snuck pillows and sleeping bags or blankets into the school. At a predetermined time, nearly every senior rolled their sleeping bags out in the hallway and promptly took a nap.

"Oh, I forgot about that." Paige laughed so hard she nearly snorted. She covered her face then, her cheeks turning pink as she peeked at Gabe between her fingers. "Remember how some of the teachers just gave up and joined us?"

"That was awesome," Gabe agreed, his eyes sparkling.

"Although I still think the trash bag slip-and-slide down the hallway would've been more fun," Bryce said with a mischievous nod of his head.

Megan laughed, noting the way Paige and Gabe had been stealing glances at each other all evening, especially when one didn't think the other was looking. They'd been friends for a long time, what was stopping them from seeing if there was anything to their relationship?

She'd love to see her best friend happy, and Gabe had always managed to make Paige smile. She could picture the two of them falling in love, getting married, and raising a family together.

It'd be perfect. The kind of future she and Paige used to talk about when they were teens.

Longing hit Megan so hard she nearly groaned.

Despite everything she'd seen with her parents' failure of a healthy relationship, she still wanted to find someone she could be herself with. The person she could trust for the rest of her life.

She dared to glance at Bryce who, naturally, was sitting next to her on the bench-style seat. If he had any similar thoughts, it wasn't obvious. Instead, he and Gabe continued to chat.

Paige leaned across the table a little so it would be easier for the ladies to talk. "I know having to stay in town wasn't the plan. But maybe we could meet for coffee before you leave again."

Megan readily agreed. "Definitely. I don't know what to expect over the next couple of days. But we'll stay in touch and get something planned. If nothing else, maybe an early coffee run Tuesday morning before I head out again."

Even though Paige nodded, there was no missing the hint of sadness on her face.

At some point during their conversation, Gabe and Bryce had stopped talking and were listening. Now everyone silently nursed their sodas or picked at the rest of their pizza.

Since the happy-go-lucky feel of the evening had passed, Megan may as well ask Gabe about the investigation. "Any news or updates on the break-in at Mom's house?"

Gabe set the crust of his pizza on his plate and wiped his hands on a napkin. "Not yet. All fingerprints we gathered belonged to your parents, you, Bryce, and the housekeeper. All of which makes sense. The housekeeper was with her daughter-in-law all afternoon. So far, attempts to locate video from the neighbors haven't led to anything. That said, the neighbor across the street is out of town. We're trying to track him down."

"And the guy from San Antonio?" The question came from Paige.

"Still no news."

Bryce dipped the last of his pizza crust in some marinara sauce and popped it into his mouth. When he swallowed, he shot Megan a confident look. "They'll find him. Chances are, he's crashed out at a buddy's place or something."

"I just wish we could get some answers." Her hand ached, the pain bringing her thoughts to the fire at the hotel. "I feel like I'm missing something here, and it's driving me crazy." She rubbed the back of her injured hand and looked forward to taking some acetaminophen when she got back to her room.

"We'll get it figured out," Bryce told her, and the others nodded their agreement.

We.

It felt good to know she wasn't in this alone. And yet, it would be too easy to allow herself to lean on this group of friends again. To depend on them. Paige was one thing, but they had their long-distance friendship down solid. It was Gabe and Bryce.

She'd felt the pain of walking away from Bryce the most, but she'd really left Gabe and all her other friends, too. How could she accept their help, enjoy their company, and leave all over again?

Megan tried to remind herself that it was different this time.

It didn't make her feel any better, though.

By the time they left the pizza place after seven in the evening, Megan was exhausted. The few hours of sleep she'd had the night before did little to sustain her. Couple that with the funeral and everything else the day held, and Megan could hardly keep her eyes open as Bryce drove them back to the B & B.

Apparently, sleep won out because the next thing she knew, Bryce was gently shaking her shoulder and calling her name.

Her eyes fluttered open, and she blinked at the B & B through her car window. "Wow. I'm sorry." She covered a yawn. "I just need some coffee, and I'll be good to go again for a while."

"I suppose you're used to functioning with little sleep at the hospital." He paused. "You know, in a lot of ways, our jobs aren't that different."

They both had long shifts, had to sleep on the job when they could, and had to be ready for anything. "You're right, they really aren't." Megan couldn't help but think about how they'd gone from being on the same page in high school, to not seeing each other for nine years, to sitting here with careers that had much more in common than not.

She didn't realize she was still staring at the B & B through her passenger side window until Bryce's deep voice snagged her attention.

"I know today hasn't been an easy day." He paused. "Are you okay?"

A humorless laugh escaped her. "I don't even know how to answer that." The day had been like riding a roller coaster—one of those where they dangle you over a drop that would surely spell death if something ever went horribly wrong. And yet, Bryce had been there with her through it all. It'd helped to have that one constant in the day. "Look, I might not have been thrilled at the idea of you shadowing me all day." His eyebrows shot up, and she raised a hand to stop him until she finished her thought. "But I'm glad you were there. Thank you."

A soft smile raised the corners of his mouth. "You're welcome." Then a mischievous glint lit up his eyes. "You should know, though, that I'm planning on staying at the B & B for the next couple of nights, too, until my next shift. Just in case you want to withdraw your gratitude."

Megan released her seat belt. "That's unnecessary. I can find my way around town tomorrow on my own. Go and get some rest. Surely there's a girl out there somewhere waiting for you to come home." All hint of humor faded from his face and was quickly replaced with surprise followed by an emotion Megan couldn't pin down. Guilt stabbed at her. "I'm sorry. That's not my business ... I appreciate what you're doing, but you don't need to feel responsible for me."

"Megan, we still don't know if there are any connections between the guy from San Antonio, the hotel fire, and the break-in. If—and I know it's a big if—you are the target, then that means they could be focusing on the B & B, too. So yes, I'm worried about you. But I'm also concerned about Erica and Peter. I'd feel better if I were close to all of you in case something happens."

That last part stunned Megan. Of course, he wasn't just concerned about her welfare. How selfish could she be? He was worried about his family.

She swallowed her embarrassment. "I'll get things tied up with Mom and get out of Destiny as soon as possible. It'll be better for everyone." With that, she grabbed her purse and got out of the car.

"Megan, wait!"

She pretended not to hear him and made her way

through the front door. She'd barely crossed the threshold when young Peter ran up to take her hand. "It's ice cream night, and you barely made it in time. Do you like ice cream?"

It took some effort to shake the melancholy mood that had descended on Megan over the last few minutes. It was made a little easier, however, by the bright smile Peter flashed at her, complete with two missing teeth in the front. Megan tried to shove her own issues aside and smiled back. "Who doesn't like ice cream? Sounds like we have perfect timing."

Bryce came inside then, and Peter launched himself at his uncle.

"Hey there, kiddo." Bryce caught him easily. "Did you eat all the ice cream? Please tell me you saved us some."

Peter squirmed out of his arms and landed on the floor running. "There is some, but you'd better hurry!"

Bryce slid a glance toward Megan, and she couldn't quite read his expression. "Erica always sets up an ice cream sundae bar on Saturday nights. Flavors vary, though. There may or may not be mint chocolate chip." He watched her curiously.

Mint chocolate chip had always been her favorite. "You remember that?" She hadn't meant to ask the question out loud.

"Of course." He reached over and gently caught a section of her hair with his finger and tucked it behind her ear. "I remember everything."

Megan's pulse thumped in her ear as sparks of aware-ness raced through her body. She barely heard his words before he moved away from her and toward the dining room. What was it about this guy? He exuded strength one moment and then was the very definition of tender the next. The combination was entirely too appealing.

It took Megan several moments to calm her heart rate and will away the heat in her cheeks before she could join everyone else.

Erica met her with a hug and an empty bowl. "I'm glad you made it. I was praying for you today." She handed the bowl over. "Help yourself. Ice cream is on the counter, and all the toppings are over there on the table."

"Thank you." Megan dished two scoops of chocolate—there was no mint chocolate chip—into her bowl, then added whipped cream and two cherries to the top.

At the table, everyone ate and laughed. Currently, Peter regaled them with the story of the fishing trip his Uncle Bryce took him on in which, instead of catching his own catfish, he ended up swimming with them.

"I'm a good swimmer. I've had lessons." Peter's eyebrows raised and his eyes widened. "Maybe next time I can jump into the river and catch a catfish with my bare hands!"

That earned chuckles from around the table. "I think it's best if we stay on the bank and use a fishing pole, buddy," Bryce told him with a wink at his sister. "You have to sneak up on a catfish, and you can't do that if you're swimming with them. Besides, down by the bridge, there are some catfish even bigger than you."

Peter's mouth dropped open. He nodded his agreement before shoving four cherries into his mouth, his cheeks bulging like a squirrel's.

Erica gave him a subtle shake of her head. Peter chewed faster, swallowed, and then popped one final cherry in his mouth instead. His mother nodded her approval, and Megan covered a grin with her napkin.

Oh, to be six again.

The thought sobered her. Being six hadn't been all that great for her. She wouldn't want to be that young girl again, hiding in her closet when her father got angry and started yelling. It'd been a blessing when she was finally old enough to go to school full time. After that, she dreaded school holidays because it meant more time at home.

She even got into trouble at school on purpose so she could stay in detention afterwards. But once she discovered how angry her father was when she got home, she never did that again.

Childhood wasn't supposed to be like that.

Peter seemed like a happy, well-adjusted kid. Even though his father wasn't in the picture, he was lucky to have a mom who tried so hard and extended family who did their best to make up the difference. Hopefully, that meant growing up would be much easier for him.

Her dark thoughts must have shown on her face because she caught Bryce watching her, a glimmer of concern in his eyes. She forced her attention back to her ice cream and, as soon as possible, excused herself.

She'd barely made it upstairs to her room and closed the door behind her before there was a light rapping. Megan paused, her hand on the doorknob. She had no doubt Bryce was on the other side. It seemed she couldn't escape from anything today. Not her mom, memories of her painful childhood, or even the boy who used to hold her heart.

Chapter Eight

Bryce thoroughly enjoyed having dinner with Megan, Gabe, and Paige. He needed to make more time for things like that in the future. Megan seemed to be having fun, too. There was a point when she relaxed, that melodic laughter of hers filling the space between them. It reminded him of the many things he'd missed about her.

And then, suddenly, it was like a switch was flipped. She'd become quiet. Introspective. And while she'd still visited at the end of dinner, her earlier mood never did return.

Their conversation outside didn't help. Her suggestion that there must be a woman waiting for him had so thrown him, he hadn't known what to say. Then she didn't give him much of a chance to explain his hesitation.

When she all but ran from the dining room after having ice cream, he knew he ought to let things be. But Bryce couldn't ignore the instinct to follow her. He had no idea what he was going to say when he got to her room, though.

Should he ignore her comment about him having a

significant other? Correct her assumption? Did it even matter?

Not in the long run. He'd watch her go back to San Antonio soon, and then he'd be right where he was a few days ago.

Except it wouldn't be the same.

He wouldn't be the same.

Megan had only been in town a short time, but it was long enough to know that he enjoyed having her back. That he'd like to have a chance to get to know her again.

The real question was whether he was attracted to what they once were, or to who she was now.

Somehow, during his mental tug of war, he'd followed her upstairs and found himself knocking on her door. It swung open.

"Hey, Bryce. Look, I'm exhausted. I think I'm going to call it a night."

The glimmer of annoyance in her eyes was almost enough to make him turn on his heels and leave her to it. But he wasn't the type to back down. Instead, he shrugged. "I figured I owed you an answer to your question earlier."

She looked confused at first but quickly shook her head. "It was stupid of me to ask and none of my business. You don't owe me anything."

Bryce motioned to her room. "Do you mind if I come in for a few minutes?"

She stepped aside and then closed the door behind him.

He claimed a spot on the small couch, and Megan wisely chose the chair across from him, a small wooden coffee table situated between them.

Bryce could feel her eyes on him as he tried to figure out where to begin. "I've never been married, and I'm not in a relationship right now." He paused. "I was engaged to a woman named Anna about four years after high school. I thought we were in love because we really got along well." He paused again, trying to figure out how to summarize what happened between them. "We were engaged for over two years. At the time, I thought she was the one. Yet somehow, we could never settle on a date. If it wasn't me pushing it back, it was her. After a while, we realized that we were only friends, and not even good ones at that. Looking back now, I'm not sure we were ever truly in love in the first place." It'd taken him years to realize that. "Our breakup was mutual. She moved away, and that was that."

"I'm sorry, Bryce. For my comment and for what happened. I had no idea."

He shrugged it off. "It's fine, Megan. Really." He nodded toward her left hand. "No ring on your finger either?"

Megan held up her uninjured hand and stared at it. "Never got close. Seeing how well marriage worked out for my parents, I guess I figured it was better to avoid it."

Between the guarded look on her face and the way she quickly tucked her hand beneath her leg, Bryce didn't buy her simple response. "I'd like to think seeing my parents together at least offered some kind of counterbalance to yours." If anything, when he was a kid, he'd thought his parents were too lovey-dovey. He and Megan used to joke about it when they were younger.

He could still remember the day he'd gone from thinking his parents kissed too often in public to wanting that kind of marriage for himself someday.

He studied her profile. "Well, I'm sure you've left a number of guys behind who count you as the one who got away."

Her laughter followed his comment, but it sounded strained. "I seriously doubt it."

"I don't. I think I can speak from experience." He hadn't intended to bring up the past. Not like that.

Pink colored her cheeks, and she ducked her chin, staring intently at the bandage on her right hand where the medical tape was coming loose. Megan tried to tuck it back in place, but it simply slid down again. "Leaving wasn't easy, Bryce. I hope you know that."

"I can understand that now. But back then... I also hope you realize it wasn't easy to be left behind, either." How much should he tell her? In a lot of ways, he hardly knew her now, and yet being around her made him relax and feel like he could share anything. Made him yearn for the friendship they used to have. "I kept hoping you'd come back. Return my calls. Let me know how you were. It was a long time before I left a store without half expecting to see you there waiting for me. Or hear my phone ring and not jump to answer it hoping it would be you."

Megan shook her head. "Bryce, don't."

"I have the right to say this, Megan. If the past repeats itself, it may be years before I see you again." His heart ached at the look of hurt in her eyes, but he pushed forward. "I thought you were the one for me, Megan. It took a while to realize that I kept looking for that in other people. Even Anna."

"So you're blaming me for your breakup with Anna?" Megan shoved away from the chair and stood. "That's not fair."

"No." He stood and skirted the coffee table until less than two feet separated them. "I'd never blame you for that. It was all me. I was trying to move on, or at least thought that's what I was doing, but I was wrong. I was deflecting instead." Bryce reached out to touch Megan's arm but pulled back at the last moment. "My biggest regret back then was not doing everything in my power to find you."

"I didn't want to be found." The words came out little more than a whisper. "My parents didn't even know where I went for a long time."

"I know. I asked them, too, that first year or so." He shrugged, feeling sheepish. "I asked frequently enough that your dad finally insisted I quit coming by the house. That if he had news to share, he would reach out to me."

"That sounds like him." Megan twisted the ends of the loose medical tape around her other index finger and stared at something on the wall behind Bryce. Her eyes finally shifted, her gaze resting on his face. "There are a lot of things I didn't handle well back then. I'm sorry."

Maybe it was silly, but her apology settled on an old wound and eased some of the ache he'd never been able to rid himself of. "We were both pretty clueless back then. We had a lot of growing up to do."

Megan chuckled—a real laugh this time—and shook her head. "That's certainly true in my case. I regret how I handled everything." She frowned again.

Did that mean she regretted her decision to leave? Did she regret leaving *him*? It shouldn't matter, especially after all these years, but it did.

As if sensing they both needed a change in subject, she held up her right hand. "I'm going to fix this bandage before the rest of the tape comes off." Without waiting for him to say anything else, she turned away and walked to the small dresser against one wall. Medical supplies were arranged on the surface.

Bryce followed and watched as she expertly removed

the bandage and then flinched at the angry flesh on her palm. "That looks way more painful than you let on."

Megan hissed as she cleaned the burn, only further proving his point. "It doesn't feel good," she admitted. Once she finished, she slathered a layer of antibiotic ointment on the skin, covered her palm with gauze, and reached for another bandage.

Without giving her time to argue, he took it from her. "Here, let me help." He fully expected her to protest, or even pull her hand away, but she didn't. Instead, when he looked at her face, he found her watching him, a mix of emotions in her eyes.

Bryce cleared his throat and forced himself to focus on the task in front of him. He carefully wrapped the bandage around her hand until the gauze was held firmly in place. He tore off a piece of medical tape and placed it, then went to tear off two more. "I've enjoyed getting to know you again, Megan. Even if the circumstances are less than ideal." He finished taping the bandage but continued to hold her injured hand in his.

"It has been good," she agreed, a degree of hesitancy in her voice. "But I have to go back to San Antonio, Bryce."

"I know." He gently ran his thumb up and down the top of her little finger. He always thought she had the hands of a pianist, her fingers long and delicate. "But maybe, this time, we can keep in touch. I don't want it to be another nine years before I see or hear from you again."

Her hand trembled slightly in his before she withdrew it. "Bryce..." She looked as though someone had backed her into a corner. Eyes wide, her gaze bounced around the room before finally meeting his again.

"Think about it, okay?" He took in her small nod and

changed the subject. "So, what are your plans for tomorrow?"

Megan thought a moment. "I'm going to stop by the dealership. I should check on Mom, too." She reached for a bottle of water and then found two acetaminophen tablets. "The sooner I can get this figured out, the better. Then Monday, I'll go into the bank. I know it's probably naïve, but I'm hoping they'll be able to help me get everything straightened out." She swallowed the medication.

Bryce mulled over what Helen had said at the funeral. Right now, Megan didn't have a whole lot to go on. "Let me know what time you leave, and I'd be happy to tag along."

"That's not necessary, Bryce. I appreciate it, though."

He wasn't going to take no for an answer. "I already spoke to the chief, and I have some time off coming. I don't need to go in for my shift until Wednesday."

"Even still, I'm—"

A loud pop echoed followed by glass shattering as shards littered the air. Megan screamed.

Chapter Nine

On instinct, Megan ducked. Bryce's arms circled around her as he turned her away from the window and pushed her to the floor, covering her body with his own. Another pop sounded. The hair along the back of her neck stood on end while more pieces of glass rained on them and bounced off the floor.

Were those gunshots? Why on earth would someone be shooting at them?

Bryce kept her pinned between himself and the floor for several seconds before finally lifting just enough to look at her face. "Are you okay? Were you hit?"

"No ... no." She gulped in a breath. "I mean, I'm okay. You?"

"Fine." He looked to the side at the window. "We need to get to the hallway. Stay low." He led the way. Once they got out of the room, he shut the door behind him. Only then did he stand again as he pulled his phone out of his pocket and dialed 9-1-1.

He reported the shooting to the police station, all the while looking her over from head to toe as though verifying that she was, in fact, unhurt. His eyes settled on a tiny pinprick of blood by her elbow and his expression tightened.

With one hand against her back, he guided her to the stairs and down. "We'll stay inside. Understood." He hung up the phone as Erica came around the corner, her eyes wide.

"Are you guys okay?" Her gaze darted upstairs and back to her brother. She lowered her voice. "Were those gunshots?"

"We're fine," he assured her. "Are there any guests upstairs?"

Erica shook her head. "No. Thankfully everyone was still down here visiting after eating ice cream."

"Good. Keep them in the dining room until the police get here."

Erica gave him a quick hug and left.

Chills broke out along Megan's arms. She crossed them against her chest. That's when a red stain on Bryce's sleeve caught her attention. "You're bleeding."

"What?" He looked confused for a moment until she pointed to the spot. He rolled up his sleeve to reveal a relatively deep cut on his bicep.

Megan touched it gently. It didn't feel like any glass was embedded in the wound. "It might need stitches." She pushed against his shoulder to make him turn, noting several smaller red spots on the back of his shirt. Her heart constricted as the realization hit home that he'd taken multiple pieces of glass in his efforts to protect her.

"They're just scratches, Megan," his voice, deep and steady, pulled her attention back to his face. "I promise, I'm fine."

She nodded, but tears blurred her vision as she tried to blink them away. "If something had happened to you..."

"Don't go there," he said. Then he pulled her into a tight hug. "We can't go there."

Though the hug was brief, she soaked in his warmth and confidence, willing herself to get her emotions in check. He was right, no good came from focusing on what might have happened. They had to look at the facts.

Bryce's words from that morning echoed back to her.

"It's possible someone tried to kill you."

At the time, his warning had seemed outrageous. She was no one special. What could she have done to make someone so angry that they would be willing to burn down a building or shoot at a B & B?

Megan could no longer chalk it up to coincidence. The evidence otherwise was too convincing.

Someone had tried to kill her tonight—possibly for the second time—and she had no idea why.

It was late by the time the police finished their investigation, took statements from everyone, and finally left the B & B. Other than two neighbors who saw a white sedan they didn't recognize, no one actually witnessed the shooting. Police dug the .45 slugs out of the wall and took them to the station for analysis.

Bryce had to watch Erica handle two sets of guests who wanted to find somewhere else to stay. Unfortunately, the hotel situation in Destiny hadn't improved much since last night. When the guests realized they couldn't find other accommodations, they finally agreed to stay after Erica offered a partial refund.

His sister handled the whole thing beautifully, but he knew this weekend was one of her busiest, and that the decrease in income was going to hurt.

While she dealt with that, Bryce and Megan cleaned up the glass in her room as best they could and boarded up the window until the panes could be replaced. Even after that, there was no way Megan could stay there for the night.

She stood in the doorway, one hand cupping the opposite elbow, as she studied the room. He came up beside her.

"I already spoke with Erica. You can take my room tonight. I'll sleep in Peter's, and he'll stay with his mom."

Megan's eyes widened. "Oh, I can't ask you guys to do that. Why don't I just sleep on the couch downstairs?"

Bryce almost told her he'd offered to do the same thing. Instead, he repeated what Erica told him. "Because it's unprofessional with other guests in the building." She didn't argue with him. "It's no big deal, okay? It's also late, so let's get your things moved over, and I'll take mine downstairs."

By the time they got everything switched, Erica had come upstairs to see if Megan was doing okay.

Megan gave Erica a hug. "I'm so, so sorry that you got dragged into this. I insist on paying you for any repairs or loss of income you have. You were so nice to take me in like you did, and all I've done is cause you trouble."

"This is not your fault," Erica reassured her. "Peter is thrilled to have a sleepover in my room. I'm even setting up his tent. We're all okay, and the police have extra patrols going by regularly. They're going to catch whoever did this." She smiled. "For now, we all need to get some rest." She turned her attention to Bryce. "And you need to clean those cuts before I drive you to the ER myself. The first aid kit is in the hall bathroom."

Bryce accepted her hug but didn't miss the seriousness

of her tone. "Yes, ma'am," he said, both to let her know he'd heard her, but also to tease her a little. Sometimes it was like having two moms, not that he really minded all that much. Still, what kind of brother would he be if he didn't give her a hard time in return?

"Good night." Erica waved and headed back downstairs.

Megan waved back. "Come on," she said, leading the way to the bathroom. "We'd better get you patched up. I don't know about you, but I'm exhausted."

He was, too. The kind of exhaustion that sets in after a huge dose of adrenaline finally starts to wear off. He followed her, then watched as she took a large first aid kit out of the bathroom cabinet and rummaged through it. She piled several things on the counter, then motioned for him to take his shirt off.

He said nothing as he lifted it over his head, only then noticing the little scrapes on his back as the fabric rubbed against them. With his back to the mirror, he craned his neck to try and get a look at the damage. Five red knicks marred his skin, but any blood lost had been absorbed by his shirt.

Megan must have agreed with his assessment of the wounds. She ripped open an alcohol wipe and gently cleaned each one. "These should heal just fine. Most of the glass bounced off your shirt. Though I think you're going to have to get yourself a new one."

Bryce turned the shirt over and stuck a finger through one of the holes the glass had created and chuckled. "I think you may be right." He tried to ignore the way her cool hands felt against his back. Her skin was soft, her touch feathery light.

"Okay, now let's take a look at that arm."

He shifted so she could get to his upper arm. It also meant he could see her face now, too. She had one corner of her mouth pulled to the side as she studied the wound. He imagined her working at the hospital, intently focused just like this, as she cared for her young patients.

She looked up and startled slightly when she realized he was watching her. Her lips formed an adorable "o" before she slipped back into her professional demeanor. She had no idea how difficult it was not to kiss her right now. Did their proximity have as much of an effect on her as it did on him?

"What's the verdict? Will I live?"

The comment brought a smile to her face. "Yes, you'll live. Though I do think you could do with a couple of stitches here."

"Not necessary. I don't care if I have a scar."

"Then butterfly bandages it is, tough guy." The words were said with a hint of affection as she dug around the first aid kit for the supplies she needed.

Cleaning this cut proved more painful than the others. When she'd finished, she used two butterfly bandages to pull the wound closed, then placed a much larger one on top of them.

"That should do it." She smiled at him, but it turned shaky within seconds. "I can't believe this happened. I don't understand why someone's doing this."

"I don't either." Bryce slipped his shirt back on before reaching for a bandage. "Let's see your elbow."

"Oh!" She'd clearly forgotten all about the small cut. She pulled her sleeve up and turned slightly.

He opened another alcohol wipe, cleaned the wound

carefully, then placed a bandage on it. He gave her arm a light squeeze before leading the way out of the bathroom and to what had been his room. They sat down at the small table in the corner.

"There's no way it's the addict from San Antonio, though," Megan said, continuing their conversation. "This is a lot of extra effort when he either could have attacked me there or waited until I got back. Why follow me here? It doesn't make sense."

"I agree, though I know Arnold is still trying to locate him. I'll feel better when we can prove he wasn't in the area for any of this." Bryce glanced at Megan and lowered his voice. "And you're sure no one knew about your home situation before you left after high school? Someone who might not want the truth of what your dad was like to become public knowledge?"

Megan's gaze shot to the door. Even though it was closed, and everyone else should be in their rooms, it was clear she worried about being overheard. "Only Paige, and she wouldn't tell a soul. And I can't imagine my mom would have breathed a word." She shook her head as though trying to jar a memory loose. "With the exception of Mom, Paige, and you, I doubt anyone even noticed my return to Destiny for the funeral."

"Regardless of the reason, it's safe to say you are a target." Bryce prayed she'd accept what he was about to say. "I'm going with you tomorrow, or I'll talk to Arnold about having an officer assigned to you. Either one is fine, but you're not going anywhere alone. Especially when we don't know what's going on yet or how far this person will go." He paused long enough for her to nod her agreement. "I'm not going to let anyone hurt you, Megan."

The next morning, Megan awoke slowly, confusion mixing with the drowsiness of sleep. It took a heartbeat or two to remember that it was Sunday, and that she was in Bryce's room. Memories of the shooting crashed in. She bolted upright and reminded herself that everyone was okay.

She'd rested peacefully last night, falling asleep once Bryce left the room shortly after their conversation. Megan breathed in deep. The room still smelled like him. She wasn't sure if the woodsy scent was his aftershave, deodorant, or shampoo, but it had a calming effect. Not unlike the man himself.

Half an hour later, Megan was dressed and going through e-mails on her phone when there was a knock at the door. She stifled a yawn before opening it to find her hostess standing there with a smile.

"Good morning. I hope you're feeling okay today."

"I am, thank you," Megan said and then yawned again. She cringed. "I'm sorry. It had nothing to do with the room or the bed. This week has been a lot."

Erica nodded. "I get it. Believe me. I have a pot of coffee on if you'd like some."

Megan didn't have to think twice. "Oh, you are a lifesaver." She followed Erica downstairs to the kitchen.

"You're welcome." Erica got a large mug—something Lorelai Gilmore would be proud of—and filled it to the brim with coffee. She handed it to Megan. "There's cream and sugar there on the counter. I don't know how you like your coffee."

"Caffeinated." Megan laughed. "And with a lot of sugar. Thank you again."

"Of course. I don't usually cook for breakfast on Sundays, but there are a variety of pastries available if you're hungry."

"I'm okay for now. This coffee, however, is amazing."

Erica beamed at her. "Have a seat." She motioned to the small bar with two bar stools beside it. She retrieved a wrapped bear claw and joined Megan there. "It's not very often that I'm up before Peter. He's normally an early riser, but being up late and camping in my room wore him out."

Megan savored several sips of coffee and observed Erica. "Peter is a sweet kid."

That had her hostess smiling with pride. "I appreciate it. He really is. I mean, we have our moments, obviously. But yeah, he's a good kid." She nodded thoughtfully as she nibbled on her pastry. "Bryce does a lot to help us, you know. Tries to stand in as a father figure of sorts. My dad, too."

"It's great you have that kind of support from your family."

"Yeah, it is." Erica took a tentative sip of her own coffee. "Peter and I are going to church this morning. You're more than welcome to join us."

Immediately, Megan started to think of reasons to excuse herself from accepting the invitation. She'd attended church regularly with her parents as a young child. She'd become a Christian at the age of twelve. But it was hard for her to go and watch her parents listen to sermons and nod as though they meant something, only to return home and act the way they had before.

Once Megan was old enough to stay home alone, she opted to do so in lieu of church. She never did find a home church in San Antonio, though she knew it was mostly because she hadn't made the effort. Something she felt bad about now.

She looked up to find Erica watching her closely. "We go to the Nazarene church on Oak. I don't believe that's the same church your mom goes to."

How did she know? Surely Bryce hadn't said anything... She must have looked skeptical because Erica held up a hand.

"I'm sorry if I overstepped. I mentioned to Bryce yesterday that I was thinking about inviting you, and he told me that you would be hesitant. I thought you might want to go with your mom, and he assured me that you wouldn't. The name of your mom's church came up." She took the rest of her bear claw out of its plastic wrapper. "You won't hurt my feelings if you stay here, either, and get some down time. I wouldn't blame you one bit."

Megan was tempted to do just that. The less she had to be around other people in this town the better. At the same time, she'd been surprised by how few people at the funeral even knew who she was. Maybe she could just go as Erica's guest. Besides, it'd been a while since she'd attended church. It might be nice.

She wanted to ask if Bryce was going but thought better of it.

"What time does it start?"

Erica smiled. "Promptly at 10."

Megan nodded decisively. "I'll go grab a shower and change, then. Thank you."

When she came back downstairs later, there was no sign of Bryce.

"Does Bryce usually sleep in on Sundays?" she asked Erica, who was straightening Peter's shirt.

"He goes over to the church early and helps with setup.

We'll see him there. He called to make sure you were coming, otherwise I have a feeling he would've come back to stay with you." She gave Megan a knowing look. "Would you like to ride with us?"

"Sure, thank you."

Peter brightened at that. "You can ride in the back with me!" he declared.

Erica laughed. "I think she'll be riding up front, honey. You've made a mess of that back seat." She winked at her son, who folded his arms and scowled.

Megan didn't know what to expect when she walked into church with Erica and Peter. She thought it might be weird or awkward.

Instead, members of the small church came forward to greet her, introduce themselves, and welcome her to the church. Erica told everyone she was a family friend who was visiting for a few days, which the people she met seemed to accept.

Any questions asked of her were related to what she did for a living or where she was visiting from. Several people commented on how they'd been to San Antonio before or that they enjoyed a tour of the Alamo.

By the time everyone found their seats, Megan felt much more relaxed. She sat next to Erica and thought it was sweet when Peter ran to sit on Megan's other side, looking at her with a big smile.

"Look, Mom! There's Bryce!" Peter stood up and waved emphatically until Bryce saw him and waved back.

For the first time, Megan considered whether Bryce would want her to show up at his family's church. His gaze locked with hers, and he smiled, putting her mind at ease.

By the time he made it to their row, the worship music had begun. He slid into a spot next to Peter and gave his nephew a knuckle bump before leaning forward to look at Megan. "Hey," he whispered.

"Hey," was all she could say before everyone stood and began to sing. Megan was familiar with most of the songs, and for the ones she wasn't, the lyrics were up on the large screen behind the pulpit.

When the music quieted, someone stepped up to pray. After that, Megan guessed the kids must be dismissed to children's church because Peter took off like a rocket, following a group of them to the back and out of the sanctuary.

Bryce didn't hesitate to shift over so that he was sitting beside Megan. "Do you mind?"

"Of course not." His arm brushed hers, sending goosebumps skipping across her skin, while the warmth of the contact seeped through the sleeve of her blouse. She swallowed, her throat a desert.

How was it possible that this man, after so many years, could still have this kind of effect on her?

She had to mentally force herself to focus on the pastor. She was glad she did, though, because he began to speak about how people are often faced with a difficult time in their life, or a difficult decision they must make. And instead of asking for help, they try to handle it on their own. He quoted Hebrews 4:16, "Let us therefore come boldly to the throne of grace, that we may obtain mercy and find grace to help in time of need." The pastor gently reminded them that God never intended for people to go through life alone. Instead, each person needs to rely on their friends and family and, most importantly, their heavenly Father.

Megan cringed at the truth of his words. She'd been like that all through her childhood and into becoming a young adult. She'd been determined to handle her family situation on her own. Even once she'd left Destiny, it'd been difficult to open herself up to new people—new friends. Now here she was, back in the town she'd avoided for so long, and it took attempts on her life to let in people like Bryce and Erica.

The need to manage everything herself? She'd always chalked that up to strength and grit. Now she wondered if she'd been unnecessarily stubborn. *I've been that way so long, Lord, I'm not even sure how to do things differently.*

She was still thinking about it when the pastor said the final prayer and wished everyone a good Sunday afternoon.

Megan stood and stretched a little. She glanced around at the small congregation and noticed Bryce and Erica's parents on the other side. She hadn't seen them in a long time, but they'd always been incredibly kind to her. Apparently, they'd already spotted her and were working their way in Megan's direction.

Mrs. Keyes immediately gave Megan a tight hug when they reached her. "Honey, it's so good to see you again. You look lovely." She held Megan at arm's length and nodded with satisfaction. "You've got to come and have dinner with us tonight."

The invitation threw Megan. "Oh, I couldn't do that. I'm only in town for another day or two."

That didn't seem to dissuade Mrs. Keyes in the least. "Nonsense. Why don't you and your mother come by? Nothing special, just spaghetti, salad, and garlic bread."

Oh, there was no way she was taking Mom to their house for anything. Both of her parents had spoken horribly of the Keyes family when Megan and Bryce were together. Megan knew it was because her father couldn't control them the way he could her. Looking back, she wondered if he'd been afraid that she might tell them how he treated her.

Bryce must have sensed her hesitation, because he reached over and touched her arm briefly. "Mom puts spaghetti in the Crock Pot every Sunday, so there's always plenty. Seriously, you should come over."

Erica nodded her agreement. "I have an assistant manager that handles everything at the B & B a couple times a week so Peter and I will be there."

Mr. and Mrs. Keyes watched her expectantly.

Well, she couldn't really say no now, could she? Besides, she didn't especially relish the idea of spending time at the B & B without any of them there. "I would love to. Thank you so much for the invitation."

"Oh, I'm so glad!" Mrs. Keyes clapped her hands together. "We usually eat at six."

She nodded. "I'll be there." When she glanced at Bryce again, he seemed pleased with her decision. He placed a hand on the small of her back to guide her to the back of the church where he leaned in close and spoke low. "I got a text from Arnold, and he would like us to go by the police station."

"Did he say what for?" When Megan turned her head to look at him, Bryce's face was mere inches away.

"No, just that he wanted us to stop by."

Bryce's words felt like cold water being poured down her back. Megan shivered and forced herself to focus on what he was saying.

"I figured we could swing by to get your car, talk to Arnold, grab something fast for lunch before checking on your mom, and then go over to the dealership. If you're okay with that, I'll go let Erica know."

She nodded. "That sounds good."

Maybe the police chief had found the person responsible for the shooting and the fire. Then all she'd have to worry about was tying up loose ends with Mom's finances.

That would be nice, but it wouldn't take away the need to go by the dealership. To say she dreaded that was an understatement.

Chapter Ten

Bryce ushered Megan into the police station ahead of him. The large reception area was nearly empty. One person spoke with an officer at the glassed-in desk while another sat in a chair waiting for someone.

Bryce checked in at the front desk himself, then ignored the curious glances he caught when they were immediately escorted inside.

"It pays to know the chief," Megan whispered, a hint of humor in her voice.

Yes, it did.

With a protective hand against her back, they made their way to a small conference room and were asked to be seated.

Megan squirmed a little in her chair and took in their surroundings. "You know, I just realized I've never been in a police station before. Either as a criminal"—she shot him a look as though she'd expected a joke from him—"or for any other reason."

"I've been regularly," Bryce admitted. "Our search and

rescue meetings are usually here. Then I go out to lunch with Arnold or Gabe once in a while."

"It really was fun eating with Gabe and Paige, wasn't it?"

Bryce ran a hand through his hair as he thought about the night before. It'd been almost like old times. So much so, that he'd had to resist putting an arm around Megan while sitting on the bench seat beside her. "Meeting them for dinner was a bit like being transported back in time."

"It was." She looked thoughtful for several moments before speaking again. "When I left, I was blinded by all the difficult things in my life then. All I knew was that I had to get away from my parents, and I extended that to everyone else in general."

"And now?" Bryce wished he had something to drink to help his suddenly dry throat.

"I can look back and see there were good things I left behind, too. But I was drowning, Bryce. I didn't know how to ask for help." Her voice trailed off, heavy with the weight of regrets she was probably putting way too much emphasis on.

"I can't possibly imagine what you were going through. Neither can Paige or anyone else. It's not our place to judge." Bryce meant it, too. "I just wish you could've talked about it more. Told me what was happening. I wish I could've helped somehow." Even looking back, it still seemed as though all of Megan's plans had derailed that week before graduation. Until then, they'd talked about a future together. Sure, there'd been plenty of unknowns. But he thought they were at least reading the same book if not on the same page.

Something happened that last week, something Megan hadn't told him yet, he was sure of it.

But now wasn't the time to ask.

As though Arnold had been privy to his thoughts, he came in with Gabe and Loki.

Bryce stood and reached out to shake Arnold's hand. "Good to see you. How's Chloe doing?" His friend had never been happier since he and Chloe Newcomb started dating six months ago.

"She's well, thanks." He grinned. "We're getting married in December."

"Hey, that's great! Congratulations. I'm happy for you both."

"I appreciate that." Arnold and Gabe joined them at the table, Loki settling at Gabe's feet. Arnold's expression turned serious as he dropped a file folder on the tabletop. "Thanks for coming in on short notice," he said, his focus mostly on Megan. "We had a couple of updates for you and figured it might be easier to speak in person instead of over the phone."

Megan rested her hands on the table with a nod. "Of course."

She looked relaxed, but Bryce zeroed in on the way she picked at her bandaged hand. She was nervous. He resisted the urge to reach over and offer her some sign of reassurance.

Arnold motioned to Gabe, who continued.

"We located the man who attacked you at the hospital. Apparently, he was released on bail." He pulled a mugshot from the folder and showed it to them. The junkie had clearly been high at the time. "He's been arrested again in San Antonio, and there is no evidence to suggest he's ever been to Destiny, much less in the last few days." He put the photo away again. "Even if he were still upset about his encounter with you, it looks like he's in jail for possession as well as intent to sell. He won't be getting out for a while."

Megan exhaled and leaned into her chair. "That's good news. I mean, I didn't think he would've followed me here. But he threatened to get back at me, and I would've worried about it when I returned to work."

That was a relief, but not a surprise. It also meant someone else was responsible for everything that had been happening here in Destiny.

"Unfortunately," Arnold continued, "we couldn't get anything helpful from the prints at your mom's house after the break-in. The house across the street from your parents' place did not have a working doorbell camera."

Gabe nodded. "According to the resident, it quit working a week prior. Whether that was engineered or a grand coincidence, it's impossible to know."

"Then we're back to square one." Megan's shoulders dropped.

"Not quite." There was something in Arnold's voice that snagged Bryce's attention. He leaned forward.

Following the chief's lead, Gabe continued the thought. "A neighbor reported seeing a white sedan driving up and down the street past your mom's house several days in a row last week. At one point, it parked across the street for nearly an hour before driving off again. The neighbor didn't catch the license plate. A similar vehicle was spotted outside the B & B at the time of the shooting. This time, we were able to get the license plate off another doorbell camera. Unfortunately, the plates were stolen from a car in Oklahoma. Still, we have a BOLO out on any vehicle with matching plates and description."

Megan hoped the be-on-the-lookout would result in someone spotting the sedan. She leaned forward to put her arms on the table. "If it's true that someone was watching Mom last week ..."

Bryce finished her thought, "...then Mrs. Bristow was originally the focus, which only widened to include you once you got to town."

"It would appear so," Arnold agreed.

"And all of it began after your father's death." Gabe gave Megan a sympathetic look.

Bryce could only imagine the mix of emotions she must be dealing with right now. Anger, frustration, disbelief. He wished he knew what he could do to help, but if she was anything at all like him, the only true answer was finding the person responsible and making sure he or she was behind bars.

Megan massaged her forehead with the tips of her fingers until her head lifted suddenly. She looked from Gabe to Arnold. "They said my father died of a heart attack. Are we sure that's really the cause of death?"

A satisfied nod from Arnold told him that the police were wondering the same thing. "It's routine to do a toxicology report when someone died like your father did. Eve —our medical examiner—ran one on him and didn't see anything unusual. According to the autopsy, he had a major cardiac event that resulted in a near instant death."

Megan stared at the table and nodded her understanding. "If they didn't kill him, then maybe his death, although natural, was still the catalyst."

"That's what we're thinking, too. Considering the different attempts on your life, this person is either simply trying to scare you or is far from a professional. If anything, most of the perp's work has been sloppy." Arnold paused as he studied Megan. "Is there any reason you can think of for someone to come after you and your mother?"

Megan's gaze remained fixed on the table. Was she wrestling with whether she should tell them about her father? She probably should. Any insight into her father's true personality might help. At the same time, it wasn't Bryce's right to share that information.

He could see her mental struggle in the way she had tensed up. When her gaze shifted from the table to focus on his face, there were unshed tears shining in her eyes.

Bryce put a hand on her arm and gently brushed it with his thumb. "It's your choice. I stand by you no matter what."

Megan blinked several times to clear the tears, swallowed, and finally looked up at Arnold and Gabe. With a slight jut of her chin, she squared her shoulders.

"There's something you should know about my dad. I trust this can stay between the four of us until necessary?"

Arnold gave her a sympathetic look. "I can promise that, at least for the time being, none of this will be mentioned to anyone else outside this room."

Gabe nodded his agreement.

Bryce offered up a prayer of peace and comfort as he listened to Megan tell the others about the physical and emotional abuse that she and her mother suffered throughout her childhood. She kept it brief and to the point, but when she'd finished, there was no missing the shock on Gabe's face or the determined look on Arnold's.

"I never knew, Megan. I'm sorry." Gabe pushed his chair back and stood. Loki sat up, his eyes on his owner, taking in his movements.

"No one did," Megan assured him. "He made sure of that. It's why I left. Why I couldn't stand watching how he seemed to care about everyone else except for his own family." Her voice caught.

Gabe's hands clenched. "I know we're not supposed to

speak ill of the dead, but if Richard Bristow were still with us…"

Arnold held up a hand to stop him. "Sit down, Harrison." Once his order was obeyed, he continued. "I assure you, the rest of us agree with your assessment." He turned to Megan. "Do you know whether your father was involved in any illegal activities?"

"No, not that I know of. However, he never spoke of legal or money matters in front of Mom or me. He did take out a second mortgage on the house, didn't tell my mom, and he's behind on payments. It's serious enough that they are sending foreclosure notifications to Mom if the money isn't paid soon." Megan released a slow lungful of air. "I was hoping to go by the bank tomorrow and see if there was any record of that money and what he did with it."

Gabe leaned forward. "I know it's not an easy thing to ask, but if Mrs. Bristow will speak with the bank and give her permission, I'll check into this for you. Besides, we tend to get more cooperation if it's part of an official investigation."

Megan pinched the bridge of her nose but agreed. "I'll see what I can do."

A surge of pride mixed with an overwhelming need to protect Megan. He resisted the urge to put an arm around her.

Arnold rapped the tabletop with his knuckles. "Meanwhile, I'll have someone outside your mom's house fulltime to make sure she's safe."

"I appreciate that, thank you," Megan said.

"What about the B & B?" Bryce asked. The thought of Megan, Erica, and Peter remaining unprotected didn't sit well with him at all.

"I can't stay there," Megan said suddenly. "All the

evidence is pointing to my family as a target. Which means, as long as I'm at the B & B, everyone else there is in danger."

She wasn't wrong. Yet Bryce could see on her face that she couldn't stand the thought of staying in her childhood home. Again, there was something unsaid there, and he wished he knew what it was.

Arnold looked thoughtful. "We'll have patrols go by the B & B regularly until this case is solved. Meanwhile, I agree we need to relocate you."

"Mom's not going to leave her house for anything. And I'm not going to hide out somewhere like I'm in the witness protection program." Megan's nose wrinkled at the thought. But something similar to a safe house was exactly what she needed.

And Bryce knew the perfect place.

Chapter Eleven

Megan stared at Bryce. He couldn't possibly be serious. "I'm not staying with your parents. That doesn't solve anything, it only shifts the focus away from Erica and Peter to your mom and dad." But a quick look at Gabe and the chief told her they thought it was a great idea.

"Their place will be safe," Bryce assured her. "Dad's land sits next to an exotic deer lease. He's had all kinds of problems with poachers trying to cross his land to enter the lease illegally, setting campfires, things like that. Dad had the whole property fenced and a security system put in place. Between that and the open fields, it's nearly impossible for someone to sneak up on their house."

Gabe nodded his agreement. "We'll have a regular patrol in the area day and night."

It did sound good. But still, Megan hated that there was a need for this at all. "I couldn't put your parents in that kind of position."

"You know my parents love you, Megan. They'd volunteer in a heartbeat." Bryce raised an eyebrow, daring her to disagree.

She couldn't. His parents were some of the kindest people she'd ever known. "I have one condition, though." She ignored the way Bryce's eyes narrowed.

"What's that?" Gabe asked.

"I still intend to drive over to the dealership and check out my father's office today. I need to see if I can find the will or deed there. Plus, Mom mentioned some personal items she wanted to get back."

They'd never get this figured out if she didn't find those documents. There was something connecting these events, and she was starting to wonder if it had to do with whatever was written in that will.

After some discussion, everyone agreed they had a good plan in place. Bryce would stay with Megan and keep Gabe and Arnold updated on where they were and of anything they found. Meanwhile, Gabe was going to start looking into her father's finances. Hopefully, Megan could convince Mom to help them out with that.

Once everything was settled, she shook Chief Dolman's hand, gave Gabe a hug, and walked out of the department with Bryce.

"I'm not going to lie," Bryce said after they'd gotten settled in her car. "I'm glad you'll be at my parents' house tonight."

"And let me guess, you'll be staying there, too." He slanted her a grin, and Megan rolled her eyes. "That's what I thought."

"Any objections?"

She thought about teasing him. Making up a reason for why she didn't want him there. But she couldn't. Not after he'd saved her life twice. The truth was, she felt safer when he was around.

Which created a whole new danger. Megan was beginning to realize just how easy it was to get used to spending time with him. Time she wasn't exactly hating like she thought she would.

"No. No objections." Her voice came out softer than she'd intended.

"Good. Why don't we hit a drive through for lunch and then head to your mom's house?"

She nodded once as he started the engine. She needed to focus on their goal today and stop thinking about how easy it was to be here with Bryce. Because eventually, she'd be leaving again. And this time, Megan had a feeling she'd be leaving a bigger part of her heart behind.

"Well, that could've gone better," Megan admitted as they got back in her car an hour later. She'd tried to convince Mom to go to the Keyes' home instead of staying at the house. Mom wouldn't even entertain the idea.

"But it could've gone so much worse, too," Bryce reminded her. "At least she agreed to sign papers allowing Gabe to search your parents' bank records."

"True. I would still feel better, though, if Mom had agreed to stay somewhere else." Once Mom became agitated, Megan had backed off the subject. "She's so stubborn."

"I can see now where you get that particular trait." Bryce deadpanned.

Megan smacked his arm good-naturedly. "Watch it, mister."

He laughed as he backed out of the driveway and began their trip to the dealership. "There will be a patrol car watching the house. She'll be safe."

Mom had been upset with her for not agreeing to stay, but Megan couldn't. When she'd left home at eighteen, she'd promised herself she'd never sleep another night in that house. She had no intention of breaking that promise now.

The last thing she'd wanted to do was explain that to Mom. Her father was gone, and Megan would prefer to forget a lot of things. Dredging them up again wouldn't be the least bit helpful to anyone. It was better to focus on what she needed to do now instead of centering on what happened in the past.

The dealership came into view ahead as though it were mocking her efforts. Nothing like throwing the past right in her face to make her realize there was no escaping it.

Megan wiped the sweat from the palm of her uninjured hand. She had only been to her father's dealership a handful of times, and it was usually for a community event. Otherwise, there was no way Richard Bristow would've brought his daughter to his place of work. It muddied the waters between home and business, and that was something he avoided at all costs.

To say she felt like a stranger encroaching on his territory wasn't far from the truth. She wasn't sure which was more awkward: this or going into his home office.

They'd barely exited her vehicle when a tall, thin man strode across the parking lot toward them. He had a smile on his face that wasn't reflected in his eyes. Wind blew his thin hair across his wide forehead. Megan suspected he was probably about her age, even though his thinning hair and frown lines made him seem older.

"Welcome to Bristow Ford. My name is Lars Simmons. Can I help find the perfect new car for you?" He looked between them eagerly.

Megan had never cared for car shopping. There were always the jokes about used car salesmen being oily, and this guy embodied that in every sense of the statement. Megan worked to school her reaction. "Hello. I was hoping we could meet with Gary Strider."

The request resulted in a slight frown on the salesman's face before he expertly brought the fake smile back in place. "I'm sorry, but he's unavailable. I'm the floor manager. If there's anything you need, I'd be happy to help you." He glanced at the showroom behind him as though he were worried someone was watching.

"I really need to speak with Mr. Strider. I'm Megan Bristow, Richard Bristow's daughter. I'm trying to help my mom get a few things settled with regards to some of my father's business details."

Lars's eyes widened slightly, and he ran the fingers of one hand through his thin hair, leaving it disheveled. "I believe Mr. Strider is in a meeting. Maybe you could come back tomorrow? He doesn't usually make appointments over the weekend."

Before Megan had a chance to speak, Bryce's deep voice announced, "We'll happily wait for the meeting to end."

Lars opened his mouth to speak but closed it again a moment later. "Of course. Right this way."

Megan fell into step behind him, Bryce at her elbow, as they walked through several lines of used cars until they reached the showroom. Inside were some of the more expensive models that Megan couldn't imagine owning. Not realistically, anyway.

Thanks to it being a Sunday, it wasn't very busy. Still,

there were a few customers milling about, and at least as many car salesmen to match.

Lars led them to the back of the showroom where three curved couches created a semi-circle facing a large screen television. He motioned to a counter, coffee pot, and fridge across the way. "Make yourselves comfortable. I'll let Mr. Strider know you're here." He turned away, paused, and turned back. "I'm sorry for your loss." With a single nod, he left, his expensive shoes clacking on the tile floor.

Megan wrinkled her nose. "I hate that being here makes me so nervous." She shook her head. "My father would absolutely despise that I'm here at all."

Bryce didn't seem to know what to say, and who could blame him? Instead, he grabbed two bottles of water from the fridge and handed her one. "Shall we?" he asked, motioning to one of the couches.

She took a seat near Bryce, opened the bottle of water, and got a drink before capping it again. "Thank you."

"I didn't realize how big this place was," he said after downing half of his bottle of water. "Apparently, your father was quite successful."

"Yeah."

Bryce cringed. "I'm sorry. I know looks can be deceiving."

"No, it's nothing you said. It's just hard to see all of this" —she swept her hand to take in everything around them— "and know this is what they judge him by. Then again, he never allowed anyone to get close. Not really. Which makes it hard for people to see the real him."

They sat in silence for several minutes. There was no sign of Lars. If Mr. Strider was anything like her father, he might try to wait them out if he didn't feel like talking to them. It wouldn't surprise her in the least.

Bryce finished his water, got up to throw the bottle away, and returned. Instead of sitting again, he did a half turn to take in the vehicles in the show room. "If you could own any car in the entire world, what would it be?"

Megan thought about the question. Around them were several cars she'd be afraid to even breathe on, much less ever consider purchasing. Outside, they'd walked past a number of high quality, although more affordable, vehicles. But she hadn't seen the one car she'd spend extra money on if she had it. The thought made her chuckle. "It's nothing here, that's for sure."

He grinned. "Come on. You have one in mind, I can tell."

She shrugged. "I'd want a 1967 Chevy Impala. A black one." When he looked surprised, she chuckled. "Whatever you think about the show *Supernatural*, you've got to admit the car is awesome."

"You're not wrong there. You've got good taste."

"Thank you," she said with a tip of her head. "How about you? Wait, let me guess. You'd like to have a fire engine of your very own."

That earned her a hearty laugh.

The clacking of Lars's shoes interrupted their conversation. "If you'll follow me, Mr. Strider has carved out a few minutes to speak with you." Without waiting, he turned on his heel and led the way.

Megan scrambled to stand and mumbled under her breath, "Well, wasn't that magnanimous of him?"

Bryce gently nudged her elbow with his as they made their way across the showroom. Lars used a keycard to unlock a door, then led them down a hallway to another. He opened it, ushered them in, and closed it again behind them.

Megan blinked at the office. She'd expected Mr. Strider to have one front and center with glass windows so everyone could gaze through them and marvel at how successful the man was. After all, that was the type of work-space her father had here.

Instead, while the office was nice with plush carpet, an impressive desk, and one of the most expensive ergonomic chairs money could probably buy, there were no windows. Only lights lining the ceiling and several plants with their own grow lights set up above them. It was much more like a fancy cave than a luxurious office.

Mr. Strider narrowed his gaze and motioned to the two chairs on the other side of his desk. "Please, take a seat." He focused on Megan. "I'm incredibly sorry about your father. Richard was a wonderful friend and man to work with. This town—and this dealership—won't be the same."

Everything about the man's voice and mannerism told Megan he was being sincere. Still, the two men had worked together for years. How could Mr. Strider not have a sense of what kind of man her father was? And if he did, apparently it hadn't hindered their friendship any.

Megan swallowed hard and tried to push those thoughts to the back of her mind. Becoming emotional in front of Mr. Strider would accomplish absolutely nothing. "Thank you." She motioned to Bryce. "This is my friend, Bryce Keyes. He's helping me tie up a few loose ends for my mother before I leave town."

"You won't be staying in Destiny?" Mr. Strider's voice was even, his expression impassive.

"No. I came in for the funeral." She avoided looking at Bryce. "However, I am a little concerned. It would seem my mom is missing several important documents that my father may have kept somewhere. I wondered if he might have a safe here in his office."

Mr. Strider looked thoughtful. "No safe, but he has two locked filing cabinets. I don't believe he ever used them for anything except business-related documentation."

He didn't extend an invitation for Megan to go through them, meaning she was going to have to ask herself. "Would you mind if we took a look?"

"Not at all. I do hope you have the keys, however. I'm afraid he never gave me a spare set."

The hope she had in finally getting some answers quickly deflated. "I don't. Is there someone here who might have them? Maybe an assistant or secretary who might need access when my father wasn't in the office."

Mr. Strider shook his head. "Our receptionist, Helen Gadd, may know, but she won't be in until tomorrow. You could stop by then. We'll be open at nine."

Megan wanted to object but knew it would only make her look desperate. "I appreciate it. Meanwhile, we'd like to look in his office. I was hoping to take anything personal home to my mother."

"Of course." Mr. Strider picked up his phone, pressed a button, and then spoke into the receiver. "Lars, please show Miss Bristow and Mr. Keyes to Richard's office."

"I'll be right there," the voice said through the speaker.

Mr. Strider replaced the receiver. "If there's anything else I can do, please let me know." He reached out to shake Bryce's hand and then held Megan's briefly between both of his. "Again, my deepest sympathies to you and your mother for your incredible loss."

Megan heard herself thank him before turning to follow Bryce and Lars back down the hallway to the showroom and the fancy office at the front. Lars promptly left, closing the door behind him. Megan took in the extravagant décor, the windows that went around half of the office, and the shiny desk. Now this was what she'd figured Mr. Strider's office would look like, too.

This fit her father, though. From the glass pencil holder to the awards on the wall. Megan's attention snagged on the two framed pictures resting on the bookshelf behind the desk. One was of her parents looking into each other's eyes as though they were madly in love. The other was her high school graduation photo.

A lump formed in her throat.

"Hey. Are you okay?" When she didn't respond, Bryce gave her shoulder a gentle squeeze. "I'm sorry, this can't be easy. No matter what your relationship with him was like."

Megan nearly turned into him, wanting desperately to feel his arms around her, but she resisted. She couldn't fall apart. Not now.

Instead, she motioned to the photo. "I don't know why, but I guess I'm surprised to see a picture of me here." She gave a short bark of a laugh. "I wonder if he bragged about me being an RN with a successful job, or if he mourned his runaway daughter." She sniffed and angrily swiped away a tear that she did not want to shed on her father's account. "I don't know why it even matters."

"But it does." No question there or even a request for more information. Just a simple statement. "Why don't I see if I can find a box somewhere. We can take those and anything else that looks personal home to your mother." He nodded toward the two file cabinets at the back of the room. "Don't worry, we'll check everything else as soon as we can."

Megan nodded and watched Bryce leave the office,

grateful he seemed to know she needed to get out of there sooner rather than later.

Bryce returned shortly with two boxes. Once the office doors closed behind him, he said, "Lars found these with his usual cheerful demeanor."

His comment coaxed a laugh from Megan. "He's definitely an interesting individual." She took one from him. "Thank you. Let's get this done."

"Why don't you take care of the desk, and I'll check out the shelves and cabinets?"

Megan agreed. That was one bad thing about an office that was more like a fishbowl. Everyone passing by could see what they were doing. Thankfully, her father also had blinds installed. She pulled them closed, giving them more privacy before they began their search.

Less than thirty minutes later, she'd filled maybe a fourth of the box with anything that seemed remotely personal. It turned out that, other than the photos and a couple of small sculptures she could picture her mother buying as gifts, there was little that stood out. With the exception of a box of cigars and a large bottle of bourbon in the desk drawer, there was nothing more of interest.

Unfortunately, Bryce didn't have much luck, either. The file cabinets were locked, with the keys nowhere in sight. Of course, if there was sensitive customer information in there, it made sense her father would keep the keys on his person. Megan would make a point of asking her mother when they got back to the house. If she didn't know of their whereabouts, hopefully Helen would.

"I think this is it," she said, her eyes on the empty box in Bryce's arms. She reached over and grabbed the fern off a cabinet and dropped it in. "Let's get out of here."

As soon as they exited the office, Lars was there to

escort them back to Megan's car. With a final wave of his hand, he turned his back on them and strode to another couple who had just parked on the lot.

They got the boxes situated in the trunk before getting into the car themselves.

He glanced at her. "You did great in there. I know it couldn't have been easy."

"I'm just glad it's over. Though we're going to have to go back tomorrow to talk to Helen and hopefully get access to the cabinets."

"Let's head to the B & B. That way you can get your things. Normally, Erica and Peter would come with us for dinner tonight, but they're going to stay put. Hopefully, if anyone's watching, that'll be enough to shift the focus off of them."

"That's a good idea. We can drop this stuff off at Mom's place tomorrow."

Bryce pulled onto the small, winding highway that led around town to the other side.

Megan thought about Bryce's parents, and a pang of guilt hit her in the chest. While her parents had been difficult to grow up with, Bryce's had treated her with kindness. She'd eaten many meals with them, and they never once wondered why she rarely invited Bryce over to join her own family. "I feel bad I never kept in contact with your mom and dad." Megan cringed. "I can only imagine what they thought of me after I left."

Bryce hesitated. "They were surprised, that's for sure. I think they figured we would stay together well after high school." He stopped there, but the rest of that sentence hung in the air between them. *I did too.*

The guilt morphed into doubt. "Maybe it's not a good

idea for me to stay there, Bryce. I don't want to muddy the waters."

He quickly glanced at her before turning his attention back to the road. "I spoke with my parents earlier, and they are excited to see you. Don't overthink it, Megan."

His words struck her to the core. How many times had he told her that back in high school? Maybe she never fully revealed what her home life was like, but at least he'd been real with her. Unafraid to say it like it was. It could get maddening at times, but it was refreshing, too.

Bryce must have realized how abrasive his words might have sounded. "I'm sorry. I don't need you second guessing where to stay until this whole situation blows over. My parents' house is the best place for you right now." He met her eyes just long enough to say, "I need you safe, Megan."

She had no response for him, but he didn't seem to expect one. His words turned her stomach into a warm mush of emotions. It'd been hard enough to keep them in check before, how much harder would it be now with them staying in his parents' house together?

Chapter Twelve

Back at the B & B, Megan studied her reflection in the mirror. After their visit to the dealership and all the emotional ups and downs of going through her father's office there, she expected to look like a hot mess. Instead, everything appeared normal. Put together, even.

Not at all the way she felt on the inside.

How had this trip to Destiny gotten so complicated? She knew it wouldn't be easy, that dealing with her father's death, funeral, and the aftermath would be an emotional storm of epic proportions.

Now someone had tried to kill her twice—and for what? It sounded like the plot to one of those detective shows where literally everything went wrong.

If that weren't enough, there was Bryce. She hadn't anticipated him coming back into her life the way he had, and he was getting under her skin fast. It'd only been a few days, and already it was hard to imagine not seeing him again.

A knock at the door drew her out of her reverie. She

expected to find Bryce on the other side and was surprised to see Erica.

"I just wanted to see if you needed any help," Erica said with an understanding smile. "I know you're staying in town longer than you'd planned. If there's anything else you need, you're always welcome to go through the clothing room again."

Erica's kindness coaxed a smile from Megan. "Thank you, I appreciate it. I picked up a few things from the store the other day. Between that and what you've already given me, I should be good." Megan reached forward and gave Erica a hug. "I couldn't have made it without everything you've done for me, though." She thought about the original room she'd been staying in. "I have a feeling my room isn't usually for paying guests."

Erica smiled. "You're right. I keep it ready and reserved for anyone who might need it. A stranded traveler was a guest once. A local family needed a couple of days after a foreclosure to get on their feet. Things like that. It's come in handy."

"I guess with your parents being willing to let me crash with your family so much back in the day, and Bryce a fire-fighter now, I shouldn't be surprised that you focus on helping people, too." Megan motioned Erica inside.

Erica sat down and waited for Megan to join her before she said, "My parents never felt sorry for you. I hope you know that." She pointed a finger at herself. "Trust me, they were worried about all the trouble I was causing at the time." The ladies laughed. "They always liked you, though. So did I. You were kind of like the little sister I never had. We prayed for you for a long time."

Erica's words simultaneously warmed Megan's heart while causing it to ache with regret. "I had no idea. I'm sorry I left town like I did—I didn't even come and say a proper goodbye." She frowned. She'd been so bent on escaping that it hadn't occurred to her that people besides Bryce might even care if she left. "I'm sorry I never kept in touch."

"I get it. I mean, I can't truly understand what you were going through. But I know what it's like to want to leave so that you're no longer under the microscope." She didn't say it, but Megan knew she was referring to having a troubled marriage and then being a single mom. "I didn't understand at the time why you wouldn't say goodbye. It was hard for all of us. But for Bryce..." She paused. "I get that things are rough with your mom. But you should know there are a lot of us who care about you, miss you, and are glad you're back." She gave Megan a knowing look. "Especially a certain brother of mine."

"He told me about Anna."

Erica didn't look surprised. "They were never a good fit for each other. Don't get me wrong," she hurried, "Anna was nice and all. But I think they dated each other because it was safe. They didn't challenge each other. Or really seem to mind when work pulled them apart." She shrugged as though she realized she might've said too much. "It was different when the two of you were together. He was constantly talking about you back then."

"It was a long time ago. We were kids." Megan absently ran her finger along the edge of the small coffee table in front of them. "Things are so different now. Everything's different."

"Yes. And no." When Megan gave her a dubious look, Erica continued. "I don't think he ever stopped loving you." She paused. "Think about it. Did you stop caring about him?"

Megan didn't like that this had been turned around on her. At first, she began to object but stopped herself. Finally, she shook her head. "No, I didn't." Saying it aloud was both freeing in a way, and confusing in another.

"I know your father's funeral is what brought you here, but maybe you can clear the air. Even if you go back to San Antonio, at least you can leave with things more resolved, you know?"

What did she mean by resolved? Megan thought back to Bryce's request that they stay in touch after she left. "I was hoping to make a clean getaway after the funeral. But ever since your brother all but carried me out of a burning building, it's been harder and harder to do just that." Megan laughed and then groaned.

Erica stood to leave. "Would it really be such a horrible thing?"

"What's that?"

"To realize that maybe Destiny has as many reasons to come back as it did to leave in the first place." She raised an eyebrow. "I'll let you go back to getting ready. I'm glad you're staying with my parents, and I hope to see you again before you leave town."

"I hope so, too. Thanks, Erica. For everything." She stared at the door for several minutes after it closed.

Megan relaxed in the atmosphere around the Keyes' table. Mr. and Mrs. Keyes had welcomed her with open arms, shown her to a guest room upstairs, and it was as if she'd never left town. Tears stung her eyes as she watched Mr. Keyes and Bryce talk about the latest high school football scores while Mrs. Keyes insisted everyone take a second helping of spaghetti, or at the very least, another slice of garlic bread.

This right here was what a normal, healthy family was supposed to be like.

Oh, how Megan had missed it. Only now did she realize how much it had mattered back in high school. If she hadn't had it to balance out her own homelife, she wasn't sure where she would be now. Would she even realize that she needed—wanted—something better someday?

She'd tried to apologize to Bryce's parents for leaving and not saying goodbye, but they wouldn't hear of it. Instead, it'd been like a time machine had transported her back to when things were good between her and Bryce. Not nearly as complicated. Normal.

There was that word again.

Megan placed her crumpled napkin on her plate and pushed away from the table. Everyone else followed suit, complete with groans about full bellies.

Mrs. Keyes reached for Megan's plate. "Dale and I will start on the dishes. Let our stomachs settle before we have dessert."

Bryce rubbed his hands together in anticipation. "Any hint on what we might be having?"

Mrs. Keyes reached over and gave her son a hug. "I made a chocolate cake with chocolate frosting. I'm going to wrap several pieces up so we can get them over to Erica and Peter tomorrow."

"That sounds amazing," Bryce said. "And I'll be happy to take the cake to them. I know Peter would be sad if he knew he'd missed out." He turned to Megan. "I think anything wrong in Peter's life can be cured with a little bit of chocolate."

"Now that's a boy after my own heart," Megan replied with a laugh.

"I'll have to remember that." Bryce's eyes sparkled as he smiled at her.

Mrs. Keyes patted them both on the shoulder. "Why don't you two go and relax? It's going to take us at least twenty minutes to clean up. Then we'll have dessert."

"Sounds like a plan." Bryce shot his mom a funny look but turned his attention to Megan. "You game?"

"Sure." Megan thanked them again for the amazing meal and followed Bryce out of the dining room. She stopped and took in the décor. "Not much has changed here, has it?"

"Oh, you think this is the same? Check this out." With a chuckle, he led her upstairs and to what used to be his old bedroom. He opened the door with a flourish and flicked on the light.

Megan stepped into the room and took in everything from the posters on the wall to the model cars lined up on shelves. "Oh, my word."

"Right? They kept it the same while I was at college. Then Peter arrived, and they figured he might want a room to hang out in when he stayed over. I don't have a great place to store this stuff now anyway, so I just left it here."

"It's amazing. Right out of the pages of a memory book or something." She pointed to the dozens of cars perched along the shelf. "My cat would have so much fun in here knocking all of those off." She laughed. "Do you have a place of your own?"

"Yeah, but it's a tiny one-room apartment. I figure, since I spend most of my time here or at the station, I didn't need something big. At least not right now."

"That makes sense." Megan went to the window that

looked past the fenced backyard to the trees lining part of the property.

"The area beyond those trees is one of my favorite places in the world. I'm still planning to build a house on some of the back acreage one day."

"That would be nice." He'd mentioned before about his dad giving him some land. There'd been a time when Megan had imagined living in a house there with Bryce after they were married.

It seemed like a lifetime ago. If she weren't standing here with him now, she might have thought it was just a dream.

And then he stepped up behind her, close enough that she could feel his solid chest against her back. She longed for him to put his arms around her and hold her, but she knew that it had the potential to change everything. Hadn't they had enough second guesses and regrets between them to last a lifetime?

After several heartbeats of silence, his hand slipped down her arm until it cradled the back of her hand. "Megan." With a gentle tug, he implored her to turn and face him. She did, and her gaze locked on their shoes, touching toe to toe, because she was afraid of what she might see if she looked at his face.

When she finally raised her chin, she found Bryce watching her, his face even closer than she'd expected it to be. But it was his eyes—and the emotion she saw there—that made her breath catch. "Bryce, this is a completely horrible idea." With a shake of her head, she tried to turn away from him, but her feet refused to cooperate.

"I'll never forget the time we spent together, daydreaming about what our future might look like." His hand fell away from hers. "These last few days keep reminding me of that. I can't help but wonder..." His voice stalled, and he broke eye contact. "You're right. This is a bad idea."

They'd spent countless hours hanging out in the tree house doing homework, griping about school, playing board games, and hiking around the property behind the house.

She thought about a spring day where they'd taken sandwiches on a hike and stopped to rest on a large stump before heading back. That's where they'd first kissed.

It'd been an awkward kiss at first—one between two good friends who hoped for more but were afraid to mess things up. But the moment her lips touched his, Megan had known she was exactly where she was supposed to be. Their second kiss had been perfect.

The memory had her swallowing hard. "Your family's home. It was one of the only places I felt truly safe back then." That and anywhere she was in his arms. But she wasn't about to tell him that. "I never wanted to come back to Destiny, Bryce. And all I've wanted since I got here was to leave again. Escape the nightmares this town reminds me of." Her heart ached at the dejection in his eyes. "Until I'm with you."

His gaze snapped to her face, the pupils in his blue eyes expanding. "What does that mean?"

"Nothing. It has to mean nothing, because as soon as I get things wrapped up with Mom, I'm going back to my life in San Antonio. I don't belong here, Bryce. And you..." She sighed as she tried to put her mess of emotions into words. "This place is your home. Everything to you. And there's nothing wrong with that. I envy you in so many ways."

"Megan." He slid a hand along her neck below her right ear, his fingers gently tangling in her hair. He dipped his head so that they were eye-to-eye. "This place isn't everything."

She felt herself falling into his words. His touch. "It's not that easy."

"Things worth fighting for rarely are." Bryce's thumb caressed the edge of her jaw, and he leaned in.

Megan tried to convince herself to step back. To disagree with him. Kissing Bryce would complicate things beyond what she was willing to examine right now.

So why couldn't she move?

The air between them seemed to electrify as his lips brushed against hers.

That's when the echo of metal grinding was punctuated by an explosion that shook the whole house, shattering the moment as surely as the sound pierced the air.

Chapter Thirteen

Bryce instinctively moved Megan behind him and led the way downstairs. A moment later, his parents ran in from the kitchen. He noted his father held the rifle that he usually kept in the gun safe. Bryce was relieved Dad had thought to keep it out tonight just in case.

"What was that?" Mom asked, her voice shaky.

Dad motioned to the doorway between the living room and dining room. "You and Megan stay there away from the windows."

Thankfully, both women moved as suggested. He saw Mom put an arm around Megan's shoulders.

Together, he and Dad moved to the large picture window at the front of the house. It only took a heartbeat to pinpoint the billows of smoke by the front gate. Bryce suddenly recognized the source.

A car had been driven into the security gate and was now engulfed in flames. The explosion had likely been the gas tank igniting.

Between the flames and smoke, it was impossible to see many details about the car itself.

Dad pulled his cell phone out and dialed 9-1-1. While he spoke to the operator, Bryce scanned the length of fencing and front gate. Whoever was after Megan was completely unpredictable, which made them all the more dangerous.

Dad spoke into the phone. "Yep, we appreciate it. We'll be watching." He hung up and slid the phone into a back pocket. "Police and the fire department are on the way. The unit assigned to patrol is two minutes out. They are checking to make sure Erica and the B & B are secure as well as Megan's mom and the officer there."

Bryce nodded, tension knotting the muscles in his shoulders. "That's good." He turned to look at Mom and Megan who were watching them from the doorway across the room. He explained the scene to them.

Mom wrung her hands together. "Do you think the driver is still inside?"

"I doubt it." Bryce suspected their perpetrator had likely set the car on fire first and then pushed it into the gate. If it'd been driven at full speed, there's no way the gate would have held. He shared his observations with Dad.

"I agree. This was either a distraction or a statement. If they'd wanted to breach the fence, they certainly could have done that." Dad hefted the rifle with one hand. "I'm going to go check the security system. Make sure everything is still in place."

"Do you have a camera facing the front gate?"

"More than one. Let's see if we caught anything. We'll be able to watch for the police and open the gate for them, too." Dad walked across the room and drew Mom in for a hug. "It's okay. We're all safe."

She nodded. "I'll put on a new pot of coffee for everyone." She gave Dad a quick kiss. "You'll stay inside until the police get here?"

"Of course."

Satisfied, she returned to the kitchen, and Dad headed for the computer room.

Bryce studied Megan and reached for her hand. "Are you okay?"

Megan squeezed his hand in return. "Whoever did this was watching me all along, just like we thought."

"And getting them to focus here is exactly what we wanted." Hopefully, her mom and the B & B were safe. He would feel better once they got confirmation.

"Right." She released a sigh of relief. "I'm ready for this to be over."

"I know. Me, too." He leaned in and placed a light kiss on her cheek as memories of her lips against his earlier caused his heart to squeeze.

"I'll go help your mom." She gave him a tight smile, then headed for the kitchen.

Bryce sent a silent prayer to protect the officers and firemen who were on their way, then joined his dad in the computer room.

Dad had leaned the rifle against the desk and had a video pulled up.

Bryce brought another chair over and took a seat beside him. "What do we have?"

Dad pulled up several more cameras on the two computer monitors. He pointed to the one showing a full view of the front gate. "The cavalry is here."

They watched as a police car and fire engine both pulled up in front of the main gate. The officer drew his gun and cautiously got out of his car, his partner following suit, and they scouted the area. They must have been satisfied because they motioned to the fire truck.

Bryce watched as some of his co-workers made quick work of the car fire.

The first police officer pressed the button on the intercom. "Mr. Keyes?"

"I see you, son. Opening the gate, come on in."

The officer nodded, got back in his car, and waited for one half of the large gate to slide open completely. The other must have been damaged by the charred vehicle because it didn't budge. By the time he'd parked inside, two more cars approached the driveway. The first officer gave directions before he and his partner walked toward the house.

"I've got it, Dad," Bryce said and went to the front porch to wait for them.

Chet, one of the guys he worked with at the fire station, waved and jogged down the driveway. They shook hands. "You couldn't make it into the station today, so you had to bring the action to you, huh?"

"Thought I'd save the commute," Bryce returned with a chuckle. "Thanks for coming."

"No problem. It didn't take much to put out, it's pretty much a charred hunk of metal at this point." Chet jabbed a thumb toward the gate. "Looked like a gas can in the back seat. Car was in neutral."

Just as they thought. Someone had set it on fire and pushed it into the gate before taking off on foot. "Thanks for the info."

"From what I hear, this hasn't been the most relaxing time off you've ever had. Be careful, man."

"Will do. Thanks again."

Chet turned to leave as the officers approached. Bryce didn't know either of them.

"Officers Krautscheid and Durant," the man said, introducing himself first and then his female partner. "We've got people canvasing the area. Is everyone okay here?"

"Bryce Keyes," he returned, and told them all he knew as he led the way back to Dad's location where the officers were properly impressed by the security system.

They watched the monitor as the white sedan came up the long driveway. The person driving it tossed something into the back seat that ignited instantly. The driver, wearing black clothing and a matching ski mask, got behind the car, pushed it in the direction of the fence, and then took off into the trees.

Bryce sighed. "I was hoping we'd be able to make an ID."

"Me, too, son." Dad leaned back in the desk chair. "Based on the way the person is walking, I'd say it's a man."

The officers agreed.

"I'm also willing to bet that car is the one neighbors spotted near Mrs. Bristow's house as well as the B & B."

Mom and Megan came in then with coffee, sugar, cream, and to-go cups.

After Mom made sure everyone that wanted some got coffee, Bryce stood and offered his chair to her. She waved him off and hurried out of the room.

Megan turned to follow, but before she did, she reached over and rested a hand on his arm for a moment. Bryce wished she'd stay in the room with them, but knew it was already getting crowded. Still, he missed her presence immediately.

Krautscheid's radio crackled, and a voice came over the air, "There's no sign of the perp. We've got some shoe impressions, size ten, but they end at tire tracks. Whoever did this either had a second vehicle waiting, or someone picked them up."

"Copy that," Krautscheid said. "We've got surveillance footage inside that we're going over now. Looks like one male wearing black clothing and a ski mask. We'll take a closer look back at the station, but I'm guessing height around five ten. Maybe one hundred eighty pounds."

Dad stood and turned. "Someone's supposed to be checking on our daughter at the B & B and Wendy Bristow at her home, too."

Officer Durant gave a nod. "Let me see what's going on there," she said and excused herself from the room. A few minutes later, she returned to let them know everyone else was safe, and there were no other incidents.

The news had Bryce breathing a sigh of relief.

It took over two hours to finish wrapping up the investigation and have the charred car hauled off. By the time the last officer left, and the security system was armed, it was nearing midnight.

Dad clapped Bryce on the shoulder. "I think that's enough excitement to tide me over for a while," he said with a chuckle.

"No doubt." They walked into the kitchen where Mom was busy wiping counters clean and putting a cover on the chocolate cake they never did get a chance to eat.

He scanned the room. "Where's Megan?"

Mom gave him a knowing look and looped her arm through his. She led him into the living room where Megan was curled up asleep on the couch, her head resting on the plush arm.

"She crashed about fifteen minutes ago," Mom said. "Poor thing is worn out."

Bryce's heart turned over in his chest as he watched Megan. "Yeah, she is. I hope she can sleep peacefully tonight. She needs it."

"I'll be praying she does."

He nodded, but his smile quickly faded. "She's planning on going back to San Antonio once this is all over. It took her dad's death to bring her back. I don't know how long it'll be before I see her again." He instinctively rubbed a tight spot in his chest above his heart.

Mom leaned in. "You know, I heard the roads between here and there drive the same both directions." She raised an eyebrow at him. "Combine that with a working vehicle, and it wouldn't be too hard for a man to make his way to San Antonio. You know, if he had a reason to go."

When Megan left the first time, he would've driven across the country to find her, but he hadn't known where she was then. He'd been tempted several times to see if Gabe could track her down somehow. But knowing she didn't want him to find her kept Bryce from making the request.

This time was different, though. He knew exactly where she was going when she decided it was time to leave.

The question was whether he was willing to risk everything to follow her and see what happened next.

In that moment, he knew that was exactly what he would do. Because if he didn't try, it'd be the one thing he'd regret for the rest of his life.

"I guess you never know, right?"

"You guys will figure this out. Your dad and I are praying for you both." She rubbed his back for a moment before giving it a final pat. "Why don't you make sure she gets up to her room where she can rest. I'll see you again before you turn in for the night?"

He nodded and kissed her cheek before she went in the direction of the kitchen.

Bryce made his way across the living room and knelt by the couch. Megan didn't move, her hands resting by her chin, her dark lashes fanned against the smooth skin of her cheeks. Her chest slowly rose and fell with each breath. He noted how the worry he'd seen on her face since she arrived had melted away. She seemed peaceful, and he regretted having to wake her up at all.

Megan's full, pink lips drew his attention. He'd barely felt the whisper of them against his own earlier, but it left him wanting more. He had no doubt they still tasted as sweet, and Bryce missed a time in the past when he would've had permission to pull her close and confirm his theory.

His hand rested against the sleeve of her blouse, the warmth of her skin meeting his. "Megan?" It took rubbing her arm with his thumb to get her to stir. Her eyes flew open in surprise, but as soon as she saw it was him, she relaxed again. "Hey. Let's get you up to your room so you can get some real sleep."

"What time is it?" She ran her uninjured hand over her face and covered a yawn.

"It's Monday," he said with a chuckle. "Almost twelve fifteen in the morning."

"Wow, I didn't even hear everyone else leave." Megan sat up and stretched. She tried to pat her hair in place. "I should help your mom clean up."

"Already done. They are heading to bed shortly, too. We should all get some rest while there's still some night ahead of us." He pushed to stand and helped her up.

She tugged on her blouse to smooth it out, made sure her phone was still in her back pocket, and gave a nod.

Bryce led the way upstairs and stopped outside the guest room she was staying in. "I'm just right down the hall if you need anything." On an impulse, he leaned forward and pressed a kiss to her forehead. "Goodnight, beautiful."

Her eyes widened in surprise at his words, but her gaze softened as she said, "Goodnight, Bryce."

Chapter Fourteen

Despite her exhaustion from the night before, Megan still woke up before the sun had risen. The moment she sat up in bed, her right hand throbbed. It hadn't felt great since the fire, but with a bandage on and over-the-counter pain killers, she'd managed to keep the pain at bay.

When she unwrapped her hand a few minutes later, she sighed at the angry red flesh staring back at her. And that, right there, was exactly why she told her patients to keep an eye on wounds. What she'd hoped would heal quickly was now going to need antibiotics. Irritated, she bandaged it up again and got dressed for the day. It wasn't yet seven when her phone chimed with a text from Paige. Megan smiled as she read it.

"Good morning! Got time for a chat?"

"For you? Always."

Megan turned the volume on her phone down so their video chat wouldn't wake the rest of the household if they were still asleep. A moment later, Paige's face appeared on the screen. "It's good to see you. How are you this morning?"

"I'm okay," Paige answered. Her smile morphed into a look of concern. "What about you, though? I heard about the explosion. Are you okay?"

Megan spoke quietly as she relayed her side of everything yesterday. "Trust me, this place is crazy secure. I'm not worried about my safety here, but I can't just hide. I'm going to need to go see Mom and address some other things today."

Paige nodded her understanding. A flicker of interest sparked in her eyes. "What's it like spending so much time with your ex true love?"

A groan escaped Megan before she had a chance to control it. She lowered her voice again to just above a whisper. "We almost kissed yesterday."

Paige squealed, and Megan smashed the phone against her shirt to muffle the noise. When she pulled it away again, she put a finger to her lips. "Shhhh! Everyone else is right down the hall." When Paige apologized, Megan continued. "He was just about to kiss me when the car hit the gate." Technically, she'd felt his lips touch hers, but barely.

"Would you have kissed him back?"

"Honestly?" Megan hesitated. "Yeah, I would have."

Paige smothered another squeal with a hand to her mouth. "Now what are you going to do?"

"I have no clue!" Megan's voice carried more than she wanted, and she brought her volume back down again. "Maybe the explosion interrupting us was a huge sign that we shouldn't go down that path. Not again. His life and everything he loves is here. And I ... my life is in San Antonio. I have a cat and goldfish waiting for me. Friends at the hospital." She sighed.

"I think we're proof that you can still stay in touch with friends even after you move. And I'm pretty sure they employ nurses at our hospital, too, you know." Paige's voice was teasing, her eyes kind.

"I'm sure they do." Megan didn't tell her that a nurse there had already encouraged her to apply for a job.

Paige studied her friend for a moment or two. "You aren't the same person you were when you left. Back then, I totally see why you did it and still support your decision. You're independent, successful, smart. You've got your life together now, Megan. I can't help but wonder..." Her voice trailed off.

"Wonder what?" Megan's chest tightened, not sure she really wanted to hear what Paige was about to say.

"I wish you could see the good that Destiny holds for you now." She shrugged. "I'm just talking out loud here. You know, making sure you see both sides of the coin. And if my best friend in the whole world were to move back to our hometown as a result, I wouldn't complain." She brought her camera closer and batted her eyes, her fluttering eyelashes taking up nearly the entire screen.

Megan burst out laughing until tears flowed from her eyes. "Oh, girl, thank you for that." She sobered a little. "And thank you for the advice. I'll keep it in mind."

"Good. Well, hopefully the police catch whoever is causing all this trouble so we can still get coffee together before you head back." Paige looked off screen. "I'd better run. You be careful today, okay?"

"I will. And you don't work too hard. Love you!"

"Love you, too!"

The screen went dark. Megan set the phone on the

side table while she finished getting cleaned up. As she brushed her hair out, she looked at her reflection in the mirror. Paige was right. A lot had changed in the last nine years. Maybe not everything was good, but she was stronger. Confident. She was Megan Bristow, not just simply Richard and Wendy Bristow's obedient, beaten-down daughter. And she'd worked blasted hard to get here, too.

Megan wasn't sure which was scarier: not knowing where she truly belonged, or realizing it wasn't as black and white as it used to be. If it ever truly was.

When Megan jogged downstairs to the kitchen, she was surprised to see the entire Keyes household there along with Gabe. "Good morning," she greeted. "Here I thought I was an early riser, and it turns out I'm late to the party." Her attention settled on Bryce who was sitting at the table. He smiled warmly.

"Not at all, honey. Come on, let's get you a cup of coffee." Mrs. Keyes was already pouring some into a white mug covered in yellow daisies and handed it to Megan. "Would you like a donut? Gabe brought a dozen over with him. Wasn't that nice?"

Megan tried to hold back a smile and turned to look at Gabe. She must have been unsuccessful because he pointed a finger at her in mock seriousness.

"No jokes about police officers and donuts. Loki and I will happily keep your share." He pointed to his partner lying on the floor. The dog's ears were straight up as he watched every move Gabe made.

Megan raised her hands. "I give up. Don't shoot." She

grinned and chose a chocolate frosted cake donut. "Seriously, though, thank you."

"You're welcome." He popped the last third of the donut he was eating into his mouth and took a long swig of coffee. Once he dusted his hands off, he took on a much more serious tone. "I have some updates that I wanted to deliver personally. Now that we're all here..."

Megan took a chair next to Bryce as Gabe began.

"We were able to go through all your parents' bank records, Megan. Your father did file for a second mortgage on your family home, but there's no evidence of that money ever being deposited in your parents' checking or savings account. It's possible he has another account somewhere in his name, but we couldn't find one. It looks like your parents mostly lived paycheck to paycheck with no activity worth flagging."

It took a minute for that to sink in. Her parents had always been wealthy. Or at least lived like they were. If Gabe's information was right, then how long had that part of her childhood been a lie, too? She wanted to ask Mom, but she had a sinking suspicion she may not have known the truth, either. "Mom has the second mortgage paperwork at the house. I'll find out who financed it. Maybe she can call and ask how my father received the money." She took a bite of the chocolate donut, enjoying the way the frosting melted on her tongue.

Gabe wrote that down on a notepad he pulled out of his uniform pocket. "That'll be great. I did find out from the person I spoke with at the bank that your parents do have a safe deposit box. We'll need the key to get in, so you should talk to your mom about that. Maybe she knows of a small key but doesn't know what it goes to."

"I'll see what I can find out. We were going to go over

there anyway, so maybe we can pick Mom up and go by the bank, too." She looked to Bryce who nodded his head in agreement.

"That sounds good," Gabe said, "I also had a thought on the way over here. It may not lead anywhere, but if the same person who set the fire in the hotel also torched the car, we may have a true pyromaniac or arsonist on our hands."

Bryce sat up straighter. "And people like that usually show those tendencies at a young age."

"Exactly." Gabe pointed his pencil at his friend. "We're going to go through juvenile records, see which local kids and teens we've had issues with over the last ten or fifteen years. With any luck, maybe a couple of them will still be in town and we can tie them to the scenes."

"It's definitely a start," Mr. Keyes agreed.

Mrs. Keyes stirred her coffee thoughtfully, a crease between her brows. "I know Bryce and Megan are going to be out for a while today. How can we be sure they won't be in danger?"

"Actually, Loki and I are assigned to be your detail today," Gabe announced with a smile. "We'll follow you over to the house and then the bank."

"That'll work," Bryce said.

Megan held her throbbing hand close to her chest. "I hate to throw a wrench in the cog, but I'm going to need to find a doctor's office or go into urgent care. My burn is becoming infected, so I need some antibiotics before it gets worse." She held her hand up for emphasis.

Bryce and Gabe looked at each other and said the name, "Jay," at the exact same time.

"He's a friend of ours and part of the search and rescue team," Bryce explained. "I'll give him a call."

"I appreciate it."

Minutes later, they had a plan to stop by Destiny Family Medical where Bryce's friend would fit her in first thing. It was a relief because she'd imagined sitting for several hours in urgent care waiting to be seen.

They went over the rest of the plans for the day while finishing breakfast to make sure everyone was on the same page. Megan called her mom to let her know they were coming over and would help her search for a safe deposit key. It was going to be a full day that Megan hoped would result in finding the will, deed, or both.

Once at Destiny Family Medical, Gabe assured them he'd wait outside and keep an eye on the place. Megan told Bryce she could go in alone, but he wouldn't hear of it.

"I can stay in the waiting room if you'd prefer," he said after she'd checked in and they'd taken a seat along one wall.

"I don't mind if you come back." They really shouldn't be there long. She reached for a magazine, noting it was from several months ago, and started to flip through it. "I was just really hoping I could treat it myself and avoid infection. It's not something I needed to deal with right now, you know?"

"When it rains, it pours?" He nudged her elbow with his, causing hers to slip off the narrow arm rest and onto her lap.

She chuckled and nudged back. "Something like that." Given everything else that had happened over the last week, the infection was the least of her worries. It was just annoying to have to take time out of everything else to get treatment.

"Megan Bristow."

A nurse called her name from a door on the other side of the waiting room. Megan tossed her magazine back on the pile and headed that direction, aware of Bryce walking right behind her. Once inside a treatment room, the nurse took some general information and let them know that Doctor Baird would be right in.

"At least we didn't have to wait long," she said, choosing to take a seat on the chair instead of the examination table.

"It helps to be friends with a doctor who can understand our unusual circumstances today." Bryce sat on the round chair the doctors usually used. He kicked off with one foot, spinning himself around twice before stopping it, a big grin on his face. "I ought to get one of these for my place."

Megan laughed out loud. She could just picture him spinning himself across the kitchen and through the living room. "I have a feeling that wouldn't be such a good idea."

Bryce stuck his lower lip out in a mock pout as the door opened. He jumped off the chair, sending it spinning toward the examination table. He stopped it with one hand and looked at the doctor sheepishly. "Sorry about that, Jay. I couldn't resist."

To his credit, the doctor just laughed and shook Bryce's hand. "Good to see you." He turned his attention to Megan. "Miss Bristow? I'm Doctor Baird, but most people I know call me Jay. I hear you've been through a lot this week. You're having trouble with a burn?"

"I am. I received a second degree burn on the palm of my hand Friday night. I've been keeping it clean, applying antibiotic ointment, and wrapping it. But this morning, I noticed an increase in pain." She tugged at some of the tape and then let the doctor unwrap it the rest of the way. She pointed to the red skin around the actual burn. "There's some cellulitis around the wounded area there. I don't see any streaking yet, though, so it's an early infection."

Dr. Baird looked closely at her hand and nodded. "I concur with your assessment." He smiled at her. "I take it you work in the medical field?"

"Pediatric nurse."

"Ah, then you've seen your fair share of burns and infections. I'll call in a prescription for a stronger antibacterial ointment as well an oral antibiotic that should take care of this infection quickly. Do you need any pain medication?"

"No, thank you. I've been fine with acetaminophen."

"Perfect. Which pharmacy do you use?"

Megan looked to Bryce who mentioned the closest one.

Dr. Baird put more medication on her hand and carefully bandaged it again. "You're doing everything right. Sometimes, though, it's just impossible to avoid infection. I hope your hand heals quickly."

"I appreciate it. Thank you so much."

"My pleasure. It was nice to meet you. I'll call these scripts over immediately. You are good to go." He shook her uninjured hand. "And you, Bryce, I'll see at the next S&R meeting."

"Yep. Thanks for making time this morning."

The doctor waved goodbye and slipped through the door, leaving them alone.

"Well, that was short and sweet," Megan said, happy to have that over with. "I hope they get the prescriptions filled quickly."

"You might give them a call in a half hour to make sure they received them okay." Bryce reached for her injured hand and brushed her fingers. "Your burn looked so painful. You're one tough lady, you know that? Not just because of the burn, but because of everything you've been through lately. You've handled it all with a great deal of grace."

"Thank you," she said, her cheeks heating. "Trust me, there are times that I've felt like falling apart." So. Many. Times. His compliment meant more to her than he could possibly know.

When they got to Mrs. Bristow's house, Baker, the officer assigned to keep an eye on the house, met with Gabe. "All quiet here."

Gabe shook hands with the man. "Good to hear, Baker. I'm going to take over from here if you want to go grab some lunch and check in at the station."

Officer Baker nodded in satisfaction. "Yes, sir. Thank you." He gave Mrs. Bristow a wave and left.

Apparently, Mrs. Bristow had been waiting for them because she snagged Megan by an elbow and pulled her into the living room. "I looked everywhere, and these are all the keys I could find..." The two women sat on the sofa and started going through the small pile of keys in all sizes.

Bryce motioned for Gabe to follow him into the kitchen where he knew they could speak without being overheard.

"Are you assigned to Megan tomorrow, too?" he asked.

"I am for the duration of the week or until the case is solved, whichever comes first." Gabe's brow furrowed. "Why's that?"

"I'm back on shift starting at seven in the morning. I was hoping to be off work until Wednesday, but we have a couple of people out sick." If the perpetrator was still at large, he hated the idea of not being by Megan's side tomorrow.

"Hey, we'll have her covered. The chief and I will make

sure of it." He gave his friend a hard slap on the back. "And if anything comes up, you'll be the first person I call."

"I appreciate it." Bryce ran a hand across the back of his neck. "I wouldn't mind filling in tomorrow if I knew how much longer Megan was going to be in town."

Gabe grinned then. "You've got it bad, man. Why don't you just admit it? You're in love with your ex." There was no question there, simply a statement that he was clearly daring Bryce to refute. But he couldn't, and when several heartbeats passed without protest, Gabe gave a victorious nod. "I knew it!" Even Loki was looking at them, his mouth open and tongue hanging out as though he were laughing.

"Seriously, man, keep it down," Bryce said in a forceful whisper. "You're way too invested in this."

In a moment, Gabe's teasing expression changed to one much more serious. "I just hate to see you miss out on a second chance that was practically dumped right into your lap."

It was hard for Bryce to argue with him. "It's not that easy, though. I feel like I'm living on borrowed time right now. She's got a lot going on, and if I push too hard, I could blow it."

"So spend time together this evening. Invite her to come have lunch with you tomorrow at the station. I'll see that she gets there and home safely. I can stay for a buffer, too, if you want. That way it's not so weird to ask."

"That's actually a good idea," Bryce said, surprised. Gabe had come for lunch several times, so it wouldn't be too much of a stretch to invite them both. Besides, he liked the idea of her seeing where he worked. He'd heard horror stories from some of the guys he worked with about women who couldn't handle the danger of their profession. There may have been issues between him and Megan, but he didn't think that was one of them. "Let's do that. Thank you."

"You're welcome. See, I got you covered. All you need to do is ask the girl." Gabe waggled his eyebrows.

Bryce gave him a friendly shove for good measure and then led the way back to where the women were sorting through keys. As soon as they entered, Megan looked up, her eyes bright with excitement.

"Check these out." She approached him, her hand held out, with several small keys nestled in her palm. "I think they might belong to the file cabinets at the dealership."

"That's great!" he said, her enthusiasm contagious.

Gabe had gone to the table to look at the remaining keys. "This one," he said, holding up a gold key, "looks like it could belong to a safe deposit box to me. Let me call over to the bank and see if the numbers on this key match their records."

Mrs. Bristow clapped her hands together. "Oh, thank goodness!"

All three of them watched as Gabe conversed with someone on his phone. When he hung up, he gave them a satisfied nod. "We've got a winner." He extended an elbow toward Mrs. Bristow. "Let's go see what's in it."

Chapter Fifteen

Bryce opened the passenger side door of Megan's car, and Mom immediately slid into the front seat. It left Megan sitting in the back. Not that she really minded, but it wasn't a surprise that Mom assumed she'd get shotgun.

As they pulled away from the house, Megan looked behind them where Gabe was driving his Tahoe with the Destiny Police Department emblem and the words "K-9 Unit" on the side. As he had on the way over, Gabe remained right behind them.

Mom turned in her seat to look at Megan and patted the stack of manila envelopes on her lap. "I hope I have everything I need for the bank." She clasped her hands together. "Your father always managed all the finances. I don't know what they'll want to see before letting us into the safe deposit box."

"You're going to be fine," Megan reassured. Last night, she'd looked at the bank statements that had been meticulously filed in one of the cabinets. Both of her parents' names were on all the documents. "Gabe let the bank know you're coming. You have the key, and you have your ID. They aren't going to think twice about letting you in."

"I don't know what we're going to find in there, Megan." Mom's voice was unusually quiet. "Your father was a force of nature. I know he didn't do right by you, but he loved you—"

"No. Please, let's not have that conversation now." Or ever. Because Mom always took Dad's side. Always found a way to justify his actions. Megan was trying to respect her mom and keep things civil.

If they opened this can of worms, there was no way Megan was going to get through the conversation without some serious fallout.

She glanced up at the rearview mirror where Bryce was looking back at her, concern etched into his features. She shook her head slightly and sighed.

Mom said nothing else, but the set of her chin told Megan she wasn't happy about being silent.

They reached the bank, and Bryce parked. Inside, it didn't take long for their small group to be escorted to a small desk on one side of the bank where someone waited to help them. Mom gave her the account number and information.

The woman, whose name tag said "Jenny," gave a quick nod and a smile. "Okay, Mrs. Bristow. I have your account information pulled up. What can I do to help you?"

Megan listened as Mom explained about her husband's death and asked several questions about their bank account. If she was surprised by the low balance, she didn't act like it. Then Mom held up the key she'd found. "I'd like to get into our safe deposit box, please."

"Of course. Please follow me."

Megan turned, but Bryce stopped her. He leaned in

close, his breath skipping along her ear. "We're going to wait over there and give you both some privacy. I'm praying for you." He gave her a reassuring smile before moving to join Gabe.

She appreciated the discretion and thoughtfulness, but immediately missed him. She had no idea what they would find, or how Mom might react. She'd feel better if someone else was there with them.

Minutes later, after using both Mom's key and the bank's to open the safe deposit box, Jenny took her leave. Alone in the small room, Mom glanced at the door then over at Megan. "I vaguely remember signing that card when we opened the bank account. I hadn't realized at the time that it was for the safe deposit box. My Richard, he was always prepared for everything."

Megan held her tongue. Her father had a lot of problems, and she could honestly say she didn't care for him as a person, as horrible as that might sound. But her mom, bless her heart, clearly still loved him deeply. Megan truly didn't understand their relationship. If her boyfriend or husband treated her like Dad treated Mom, Megan would be out of there fast enough to make his head spin. After kicking him where it hurt.

Mom ran a shaky hand over the top of the metal box. "Let's see what's in here." Megan stood next to her as she lifted the lid. They both peered inside.

Megan had imagined all kinds of things ranging from piles of money to a little black book. What they found were birth and marriage certificates, photos of his parents, even some photos of her as a baby along with her parents' wedding.

There were several pieces of jewelry. Mom reached in and carefully extracted a delicate gold chain complete with a tiny cross. "This was Richard's mother's," she said, just above a whisper. "I had no idea he still had it." She put it back on the small velvet tray inside.

With a sad smile, Mom picked up a ring with a large diamond on it. "After I got pregnant with you, my fingers swelled, and I couldn't wear this ring anymore. My fingers never did go back to their regular size. Your father bought me a new ring, saying it was better to do that than to resize this one. He didn't want to risk it being damaged." She held her left hand out for emphasis. "I assumed he sold this ring to pay for it. I had no idea he'd kept it all these years." A tear made its way down her weathered face, and she wiped it away with a single finger. "Your father was a hard, difficult man sometimes. But he loved fiercely."

It took everything in Megan to keep quiet. She had no doubt her father loved Mom and even her in his own way. But there was a difference between love and respect. Between caring for someone and controlling them. Megan had witnessed her father hit Mom too many times to believe that his love made up for that.

She'd had enough of this convoluted trip down memory lane. "But no will or deed."

"No." As though the bubble had been burst, she put the ring back in the box and closed it with finality. She gave Megan a sad look. "I can't lose my house, Megan. I can't."

"I know, Mom." There were a lot of things she didn't understand, but she knew her mom didn't deserve to lose everything. Not all at once like this. "We're going to get this figured out. I know we will."

"Was today as exhausting for you as it was for me?" Megan asked as Bryce pulled through the security gate and up to the driveway of his parents' house. "It feels so much later than just five-thirty."

"It was a lot for one day," he agreed. Even though the events of the day weren't things he might have chosen to do, spending that time with Megan had made it more than worthwhile. On the way back to his parents' house, they'd stopped to get her antibiotics from the pharmacy and then picked up burgers from the best place in town. "And I am starving. Those sandwiches at lunch didn't go far."

"No, they didn't. It'll be good to just relax a little tonight. I'm going to run upstairs and change clothes before dinner."

"Sounds like a plan." They carried bags of food inside the house, were welcomed by his parents, and then Megan disappeared.

"Was everything quiet today?" he asked his dad, who assured him nothing unusual had happened.

Bryce was glad, but after the car fire the night before, and everything else that had been happening, the lull in activity felt weighted. Whoever was behind this wouldn't just give up and walk away. Which meant they were planning something. That unknown was what prevented Bryce from relaxing.

He'd texted with his parents earlier to let them know his plans for dinner. They brought plenty of food for his parents to eat, but Bryce thought he and Megan would eat in the tree house instead. It might be a bit of a crazy idea, but he wanted to spend some time alone with her. Try to get a sense of how she was feeling about him. About them. Besides, the tree house held a lot of great memories of time spent together. Maybe the nostalgia would be good for both of them.

When Megan came back downstairs, she stopped and stared at the large basket he had in his hands. "What's that?"

"Since I go back on shift first thing tomorrow, I thought we could have a picnic for dinner. I've got the burgers, sodas, and even a portable DVD player and a selection of movies to choose from. If you're game, that is." He really hoped she would be, but added, "If you'd prefer to eat here, that's fine, too," just in case she was truly tired, or her hand was bothering her.

To his relief, she nodded her agreement. "That sounds like fun. Thank you. I'm assuming we're staying close by?"

"Very close. You'll see." He grinned at her, then led the way out the back door.

He heard Megan take in a deep breath. "It always smells so good out here," she said. "When we were kids, it was like this place had a bubble of peace surrounding it, unaffected by everything else."

"Safe." It was that way for him, too. He led the way across the large, fenced backyard to a line of trees.

"Here we go," Bryce said and came to a stop. He grinned at Megan and motioned ahead of them.

She gasped when she looked up and saw the tree house. "It's still here!"

Bryce remembered the first time he'd showed it to her. He and his dad had spent several weekends building it together. After that, he and Megan were frequent visitors.

"It looks a little smaller now, doesn't it?" Her voice sounded wistful.

"A little. I'm glad that storm we had last year didn't take it out." He raised his eyebrows. "Shall we?" Without waiting for her answer, he climbed the ladder as he balanced the picnic basket in one hand. "Be careful, two of the rungs need to be replaced. I didn't realize that until now." He glanced down to see she was poised to follow him.

Megan made it past the last broken rung and stumbled over the threshold of the tree house. Bryce grasped her arm just above the elbow to steady her. The motion changed her trajectory. She caught herself mere inches from bumping into him and braced her uninjured hand against his chest. Her palm might have been an iron the way her warmth seemed to brand his skin. "You okay?"

She nodded and cleared her throat before stepping back again.

"I'll be sure to fix that ladder. If for no other reason, to make it safe for Peter. I can see him playing up here soon." He had no doubt his young nephew would enjoy the tree house for years to come.

He spread a thick blanket out on the wooden floor before they worked together to set the food and drinks on it. When Megan sat down herself, she let out a groan. "Oh, the food smells amazing. I can't remember the last time I had a good cheeseburger."

Bryce blinked at her. "What do you normally eat back in San Antonio? Please tell me you haven't become one of those salads-only types."

She laughed hard at that. "No, nothing like that. I just tend to either eat simple meals at my place, or I eat at the hospital cafeteria. And let me tell you, they can make a lot of great food, but a quality burger is not on that list." Bryce watched as she took her first bite, her eyes closing as she nodded appreciatively. "So good. Thank you."

"You're welcome." He took a bite of his own burger and had to agree it hit the spot. They ate in comfortable silence for several minutes before he started up another conversation. "What do you do for fun back home?"

Megan hesitated for a moment. "I spend a lot of my free time at the hospital, I guess. It's hard because we have some kids that are there on a more long-term basis. I get so used to seeing them during my shifts that I wonder how they're doing when I'm home. If I'm ever living somewhere besides an apartment, I'd like to get a dog and train it to come with me to visit the kids." Her entire demeanor brightened as she spoke about her future plans. "I tried to convince my cat to become a therapy animal, but he didn't like the idea too much." She laughed. "So Smokey stays home with my goldfish, Sushi."

Bryce was just about to eat another French fry but set it back down again. "You have a goldfish. Named Sushi." He grinned. "I am having the hardest time imagining that. And what inspired you to choose a name like that instead of Bubbles or Goldie?"

"When I first got the fish, Smokey wouldn't stop watching it while licking his lips. I wasn't sure if it would survive my first shift at the hospital or if Smokey would catch and eat it. I named the poor thing Sushi. Morbid, I know. But it's been a year, and they've managed to get along okay."

He laughed again. "That's awesome."

He wondered what her apartment looked like. He tried to picture her there, happily lounging on a couch reading her book, but it seemed like a scene from an entirely different world. The thought pulled the corners of his mouth down before he realized it.

"What's wrong?"

"I wish I didn't have to go back on shift tomorrow." Not a lie, he was worried about that, too. But yeah, he was totally deflecting. "I don't like that someone wants to hurt you, and I can't be here to watch your back."

"Gabe will stay close. We'll be fine. Besides, we're bound to get a break in the case soon, right?"

"I'm sure you're right."

They finished eating their food. Bryce cleaned everything up and then handed her a chocolate mint the restaurant was famous for including with their meals. He ate one himself, allowing the chocolate to melt in his mouth. "It's almost worth going there just for the candy."

Megan shifted so that her back was against the wall of the tree house. "It is good," she agreed. She finished her treat and pulled her knees to her chest, looping her arms around them. "I've missed this, Bryce. Talking to you. Everything seemed so much easier when we came up here. School, people, just life in general." She looked around the small area. "I'm glad you guys left this here. It's neat to think that Peter will grow up having a place like this to play in."

"I'm really glad he will, too." He took his cue from her and leaned against the same wall, his right arm brushing up against her left. But after a few minutes of silence, he shifted so that he faced her. "Can I ask you for a favor?"

She seemed surprised. "Sure. I think I owe you at least one after everything you've done for me over the last few days. What is it?"

He swallowed past the lump in his throat. "When the case gets wrapped up, promise me you won't leave town this time without saying goodbye."

The invisible weight that lifted from his chest after finally voicing his worry seemed to settle right onto her shoulders. "Bryce..."

"After reconnecting like this, I can't just let you disappear again." He released a quick breath. There. It may not be everything he wanted to say, but at least it was a start.

Megan stood then and walked to the small window. It used to look out over the yard, but the tree had grown enough that branches and leaves blocked their view. Still, she stared as though there was something interesting to see.

Bryce stood, too, and it took everything in him to not reach out and touch her. Instead, he buried his hands in his pockets.

"I promise I won't leave without seeing you first."

Her words eased some of his trepidation about tomorrow. "Thank you." He thought about stopping there, but he couldn't. "You should know I never quit caring about you, Megan."

Without turning around, she said, "You're not going to make leaving easy, are you?"

Bryce shifted to her side and reached for her hands, taking care not to bother her burn, and gently tugged her around to look at him. "I'm serious about wanting to keep in touch even after you go home. I guess what I need to know is whether you feel the same way." Bryce traced soft circles on the backs of her hands with his thumbs.

She seemed to look everywhere but at him—his shirt, their shoes, their joined hands. Finally, she raised her chin, and those gorgeous hazel eyes of hers fixed on his face. "I never stopped caring about you, either."

He released the breath he hadn't realized he'd been holding. Gently, he cupped her jaw with one hand, brushing the corner of her mouth with his thumb. Bryce wanted to kiss her with every fiber of his being, and in that moment, all that seemed to exist were him, Megan, and their separate paths that were so close to intersecting it made his chest hurt.

He leaned toward her and was elated when she met him partway, closing the distance in a kiss he'd long imagined and never realized could be so amazing. Everything about it from the way her lips moved against his to how her arms felt looped around his neck was perfection. Like a page out of their history book, but even better. The kiss was brief, and when he opened his eyes to study her face, her lashes fluttered and lifted.

Her eyes held a need that he knew reflected his own. But there was also worry and confusion. Emotions he wished he could ease but didn't know how.

"Bryce? What are we doing?"

"I wish I had all the answers, Megan." He let his forehead rest against hers. "For now, I think we're going to have to take it a day at a time."

When Megan nodded and gave a little sigh, he pulled her closer and kissed her again. This time, he poured his heart into the kiss until it left them both breathless.

She turned away from him to face the window again, and he wrapped his arms around her waist while resting his chin on her shoulder.

He groaned. "I can't stay at my parents' tonight. I need to go home, do some laundry, and get ready for my shift tomorrow. I'm going to miss seeing you in the morning."

"I'm going to miss you, too," she said, placing a hand over his.

"I've gotten used to seeing you every day now. I wondered if you might come have lunch at the station tomorrow. You can meet some of the people I work with." Before she could object, he went on to reassure her that Gabe was coming, too, and did so regularly.

"Are you sure I won't be intruding?"

"Absolutely."

"Then I'd like that." She shivered a little, and only then did Bryce notice the chill settling in the air.

"Come on, let's get back inside before it gets too cold."

He desperately wanted to protect her. From the cold, from the sadness of the world, from someone who wanted to kill her. All he could do was pray that his efforts would be enough.

Chapter Sixteen

At Destiny Fire Department, Chet gave Bryce a knowing look. "Your ex is in town, and you invited her to come by and have lunch with us today." There were all kinds of innuendo hidden in his words. "That doesn't sound like nothing, man."

Bryce grumbled and raised both of his hands. "Clearly, I made a mistake asking an old friend to swing by before she leaves town again." He looked around the table at his friends and colleagues as they ate breakfast.

It's not like having friends or family join them for a meal was unusual. Bryce's parents and even Erica and Peter had come by before.

But this was the first time he'd invited a woman to join him. At least since his ex-fiancée. It was a big deal, and everyone else knew it. They also knew he was joking with them as much as they were teasing him.

"She's just in town for a few days. Seriously, please don't make it a big thing."

"Does she know it's your turn to cook?" Leslie, the only woman on shift, said from the other side of the table. "That might be enough to send her running. Now if Henry were here..."

Bryce stuffed a bite of pancake in his mouth and then pointed the fork at her. "Funny," he said after he'd chewed and swallowed. Henry, the guy he was filling in for, was a crazy good cook.

Truthfully, he half expected Megan to cancel. Since her time in Destiny was limited, it was killing him not to be with her now. Throw in the fact that someone out there could still be targeting her, and he couldn't help but worry.

Bryce resisted the urge to text her and see how things were going.

After breakfast, Bryce and Chet worked together to clean up the mess. "They figure out who's trying to hurt your girl yet?" Chet asked.

Megan technically wasn't his girl, but he didn't correct Chet. "Not yet. We've got a few leads, evidence that seems random and unconnected, and a motive that isn't overly clear yet."

"That's rough."

"Yeah, it is." He finished the dishes and dried his hands on a towel. "We're missing something. Something big, and it's driving me crazy." Bryce lowered his voice. "Every time we get a call, I think about the call out to the hotel and finding Megan there."

"And you worry it'll have something to do with her again."

Bryce nodded.

"All any of us can do is focus on our jobs and trust it'll work itself out. Sounds like she's pretty good about taking care of herself."

With a chuckle, Bryce had to admit he was right. "She's tough, that's for sure."

It was a relatively slow day with only one call to assist with a car accident, and another to put out a small structure fire thanks to a campfire set too close to a shed. They were back in plenty of time for Bryce to set up lunch.

It wasn't that fancy. He'd gotten all the fixings for submarine sandwiches, including several kinds of meat, cheeses, and a variety of veggies. He set them out buffet-style, opened large tubs of potato and macaroni salads, and made sure the fridge was stocked with drinks.

To his surprise, ten minutes before lunch, Chet came into the kitchen with people in tow. "Look who I found wandering around the bay."

Megan waved but looked uncertain as she hung back near Gabe. Hopefully, Chet hadn't been too obnoxious when she said who she was. "Hey. I hope it's still okay that I came by."

"Absolutely." He shook Gabe's hand and gave Megan a hug, breathing in the fresh scent of her shampoo. "Did you officially meet Chet?"

Chet gave him a mock-offended look. "I introduced myself like a proper gentleman, thank you very much." He raised an eyebrow at Megan. "You see what I have to deal with around here?"

Megan chuckled in response as the rest of the crew trickled in. Once they were all there, Bryce cleared his throat. "Guys, this is Megan, a good friend from high school." He then introduced everyone. They already knew Gabe, who hadn't hesitated to start making a sandwich.

Thankfully, his co-workers were super polite as they welcomed her, expressed their condolences for her father's passing, and said they were glad she wasn't hurt worse in the fire.

"I could tell right away it was arson," Chet said as he

piled his sandwich high and added a more than generous amount of mayonnaise. "Fires usually have a personality. It's hard to explain."

Megan took her sandwich to the table and sat down, a can of Sprite resting near her plate. "I still don't understand why someone is after me in the first place." Her gaze locked with Bryce's for several moments before she blinked and looked away. "Do you guys deal with arson very often?"

"You'd be surprised." Gabe swallowed his mouthful and spoke again. "People think they can set a fire and collect the insurance money."

Leslie nodded. "It's true, but really the number of fires that are set intentionally is small." She picked up a piece of bell pepper and popped it into her mouth. She narrowed her eyes as she studied Megan. "I'm sorry that happened to you, though. I hope they catch whoever is responsible."

"I appreciate that."

Bryce finished making his sandwich and took a seat next to Megan. They began to eat, the conversation laid back as they answered Megan's questions or just talked in general about what each of them had planned for their vacation time.

Megan dusted her hands off when she'd finished her sandwich. "Well, I want to thank you for what you guys do. I can say firsthand that you are all saving lives out there." She glanced at Bryce. "Even if I'm still amazed that you let this guy into the fold."

Bryce's neck grew warm as everyone around the table roared with laughter.

Chet pointed at her and announced loudly, "I like her."

Bryce watched as Megan conversed with his co-workers and friends. She seemed to fit right in, as though she'd been coming by for meals all along.

Like she belonged there. Belonged with him.

As if she could somehow hear his thoughts, her beautiful eyes shifted to lock with his. The smile she offered just for him had his pulse jumping into overdrive.

When he got done with his shift, he had every intention of making sure she knew how much he wanted her in his life—no matter what he had to do to make that happen.

An alarm went off, piercing the air with its insistence. As soon as he heard Battalion 2, Bryce jumped up from his chair. "That's us." He gave Megan an apologetic look. "I'm sorry. But I'll call you later, okay?"

"Yeah, okay. Be safe?"

He smiled at her. If it weren't for their audience, he would have leaned in and kissed her again. "Always."

Megan had no idea what to expect from meeting Bryce for lunch at the station. All of his co-workers had been friendly and welcoming. It didn't hurt that Gabe was there to break the ice and keep the conversation going. And with Leslie in the room, Megan wasn't even the only woman.

In the end, she didn't feel at all like an outsider. It was nice to see where Bryce worked and get a sense of the fire station atmosphere.

Megan had jumped a foot when the alarm initially sounded. It was interesting to see how all the firefighters around the table listened intently and then jumped into action. Gabe had warned her ahead of time, so at least she'd known it was a possibility. Apparently, Bryce had been called out more than once in the past while Gabe was there for a meal.

Pride filled her chest as she'd watched their engine leave

the station. She knew well that adrenaline surge when a patient came into the ER needing help. Is that how Bryce felt when he was sent out on a call?

She tried not to think too hard about the fact that a structure fire had been announced. Would it be something that Bryce and his team could put out easily? Or would he have to go inside to fight the fire?

Gabe interrupted her introspection. "Why don't we put all of this away for them? Someone else will be up here shortly, but we have a few minutes."

Megan took in the sandwich fixings and nodded her agreement. She regarded Gabe as she wrapped up the cheeses. "So how come you haven't gotten married and settled down?"

The question must have surprised him because he paused in the middle of putting sliced veggies into a plastic container. He covered his reaction quickly with a smile. "Why? Are you offering?"

"Funny." She smacked him in the arm, and they both laughed. "I was thinking about you, me, Bryce, and Paige. You'd think at least one of us would have the white picket fence and all that by now."

Gabe looked at her thoughtfully. "I don't know. I mean, my job with the police obviously comes with some risks, but I know plenty of officers who have families. I guess it's all about finding the right person, you know? Even then, we can talk about the potential risks that go along with what I do, but I also realize that going through a situation if I'm injured, God forbid, is a lot different than talking about it." Gabe finished with the veggies and moved on to the bread. "Why do you ask?" He glanced at her curiously, but there was something in his eyes that told Megan he knew exactly why she'd ventured into this line of questioning.

When she didn't respond, he placed the wrapped sandwich bread in a cabinet, then turned to look at her. "The fact is, until we're faced with a situation, none of us can really know how we'll respond. But if you truly accept another person for who they are—including what that person is called to do—then you accept the good and bad that goes with it. The risks and the rewards." His usual laid-back smile returned to his face. "Then hopefully, the rewards far outweigh the risks. At least theoretically."

Megan blinked at him. "Since when did you become so mature and well spoken?" What he said made so much sense. She knew it wasn't simple, but he made it sound like it could be.

And then her goofball friend returned with a big grin and an exaggerated shrug. "It comes and goes."

"That's kinda what I figured. Any chance some of that sage advice might be used to help you communicate with a certain mutual friend of ours?"

From the slight reddening of his neck, it was clear Gabe knew she was referring to Paige. "I could pose a similar question to you. Is it possible for a pediatric nurse and a certain firefighter we both know to find some middle ground?" The tone of his voice suggested he was teasing, but the kind look in his eyes told her he was legitimately concerned about his friends.

"We're quite the pair, aren't we?" Megan wiped off the counters. "Let me survive the next day or two, you catch an attempted murderer, and then we can worry about the future. Deal?"

"Deal."

She was joking, but as Gabe escorted her to his Tahoe where Loki waited, he stayed by her side and remained alert to their surroundings.

He unlocked his Tahoe and held the passenger door open for her. Megan welcomed the cool air inside. She looked over her shoulder through the grated window at Loki standing in the kennel area behind the seats.

Gabe opened the back door and gave Loki a hearty pat along with a treat. "Good boy!" he praised. The dog responded with tail wags that drummed against the side of his kennel.

Megan smiled at the scene. There was no doubting the bond the two of them had. Riding with them this morning made her feel safe. No one in their right mind would want to risk coming face-to-face with a German shepherd like Loki.

Gabe closed the kennel, took another look around the parking lot, and got in.

Megan sobered. His actions were a reminder of how serious things had become. She hated that her friends were having to put their lives on the line to protect her.

Chapter Seventeen

After leaving the fire station, Megan and Gabe swung by Mom's house. Megan ran inside to get the information about the company holding the second mortgage and gave it to Gabe.

She then got in her car and, with Mom settled in the passenger seat, they headed for the dealership with Gabe following them in his Tahoe.

She looked over at Mom who seemed especially fragile today, her skin pale. "If you're not up to this, I can go on my own. Some extra rest would do you good."

A sigh escaped Mom's lips. "If I spend another minute resting alone in my house, wondering whether I'll be living there in a month, I'll go insane." She patted her hair. "Besides, I should speak to Gary and make sure he's okay with continuing to manage the dealership now that my Richard is gone."

Megan said nothing as they continued their drive. Once they arrived at the dealership, Lars seemed to appear out of nowhere again. However, whether it was due to their previous visit or the fact that Gabe was with them, he didn't question them about why they were there. The only hint of disapproval was when he observed Loki with a frown before leading the way to Dad's office.

Mom stalled in the doorway for several heartbeats before going inside. How many times had she been here? Megan hoped the fact that they'd already retrieved all the personal items might make it easier.

Lars hesitated, looked like he wanted to say something, and then left them alone.

They shut the office door behind him, and Megan closed all the blinds again.

She hadn't known what to expect from Mom, but a few moments of silence were followed by a determined nod of her head. She pulled the small keys out of her pocket. "Let's find what we came here for."

Gabe's eyebrows rose, and Megan only shrugged in response. She'd been more likely to bet on an emotional outburst than cool composure.

Together, they went through everything in the cabinets file by file. Helen ducked her head in and asked if they'd like some coffee, which all of them happily accepted.

After two hours of mostly silence punctuated by communication from Gabe's radio, almost everything they found was either customer-specific or related to the stock they had on the lot.

"Mr. Strider was right, it doesn't look like he kept anything personal in here," Megan mused.

Mom let the file she was going through flop on top of the desk with a sigh just as Gabe's phone rang.

"It's the station," he told them as he answered. "Harrison here."

Megan and her mom watched as Gabe held a short conversation before he hung up again.

He pocketed the phone. "We tracked down the company that financed the second mortgage on your home, Mrs. Bristow. It's based out of the Dallas area. The money was sent electronically to a bank account that your husband gave them. Unfortunately, they refuse to release account numbers until we get a warrant. The chief is working on that now."

"I don't understand why he didn't tell me any of this." There was no missing the sadness in Mom's eyes. "I wish he had." She looked at Megan then, imploring her to explain why her entire world had turned upside down in the course of a week.

Megan glanced at Gabe who, thankfully, understood what they needed.

He called Loki to his side. "Why don't we step outside and make a few more calls? I'll be within sight." He motioned to a seating area not far from the office door.

As soon as they were alone, Megan pulled another chair over and sat down. It took everything she had to not voice the words that echoed in her head. "Maybe there were financial concerns, and he didn't want to worry you." *Or he wanted to continue to control you. Like he had your entire marriage.* She wanted to scream the truth, but Mom had never been able to admit her husband's flaws before. Now that he was gone...

"I'm not an idiot," Mom said, barely above a whisper. She ran a hand over the large desk in front of her, her gaze unfixed. "I know your father had issues. I chose to live my life with him. To accept his flaws. To forgive over and over again." Her eyes lifted, pain overriding every other emotion. "But you didn't have that choice. I'm sorry, Meggie. I'm sorry I wasn't a better mother, that I didn't protect you like I should have."

It was the last thing Megan had ever expected to hear. The words hit her like a ton of bricks, causing tears to spring to her eyes even as she willed them away. How many times had she wished her mom would stand up to him, insist that he treat them both better?

"Dad was abusive. I grew to accept that, to expect that of him." Megan hardly recognized her own voice. "There are so many times I can look back and wonder why I didn't report him. Especially when he got angry with you and left bruises. Maybe I could've put a stop to it."

Mom shook her head and held up a hand. "No. You can't blame yourself. You know as well as I do that no one would have believed you. I would never have pressed charges." She took a deep breath. "You got out of here as fast as you could, and it's exactly what you should have done." Tears began to fall, chasing each other down her cheeks.

"I hated leaving you behind, Mom. But you wouldn't walk away, and I couldn't keep watching him treat you like he did. Then watch everyone who knew him fawn all over him like he could do no wrong." There was no keeping her own tears back now. She allowed them to fall, unhindered.

"You are so much stronger—and braver—than I could ever hope to be." Mom reached for Megan then, and she allowed herself to sink into her mom's embrace, something she hadn't done since she was a little girl.

Megan leaned back and grabbed two tissues from the box on a back table. She handed one to Mom and used the other herself. "I'm sorry for your loss, Mom. And for the mess Dad left behind in his wake. But I truly hope this might mean the start of a life you've always deserved." Maybe even a renewed relationship between them. Some of the pressure that gripped her chest every time she thought about Dad eased.

Mom dabbed at her eyes and gave her daughter a shaky smile.

Megan thought about Bryce and wanted to tell him what had just happened. He'd be as shocked as she was—and happy, too. She took in a sharp breath as she realized that many of her reasons for leaving Destiny were slowly melting away.

A soft knock on the door drew Megan's attention. She blew her nose, hoped she didn't look like too much of a mess, and opened it. Gabe stood outside. As soon as he saw her face, his expression turned to one of concern.

"We're good," she assured him in a whisper.

"I'm glad." He used his thumb to point behind him. "I happened to run into Mr. Strider, and he has some information I think you and your mom need to see."

Megan nodded and opened the door wider. Gabe and Loki entered followed by Mr. Strider.

The older man seemed to take in the stacks of files and the heavy emotional feel of the room. "I spoke with Officer Harrison. I didn't realize Richard hadn't kept you updated on financial aspects of the business." He sat in the chair opposite Mom and laid some papers on the desk between them. "A year ago, Richard came to me and offered to sell me half of the dealership, making us partners, with the agreement that the business would keep his name. Since it was so successful, I didn't see any reason to argue otherwise."

Megan watched as he showed Mom the papers they'd drawn up, proving that he owned half of the dealership. Everything seemed to be legitimate. "How did you pay my father? We've found no evidence of large amounts of money being deposited into his bank account."

"It was unusual, but Richard did ask me to pay him by

cashier's check. I had no reason not to. I don't know what he did with the money once he received it."

Another dead end. Either he used all the money, or he kept it somewhere. Like Mom had pointed out the other day, Dad liked to keep his assets close. The money—or evidence of what happened to it—had to be at the house. Somewhere.

Mom finally released the tissue she'd been holding and dropped it into the wastebasket by her feet. "Thank you for the information, Mr. Strider. Your help has been invaluable."

Mr. Strider leaned forward earnestly. "I will do everything in my power to help when it comes to managing Richard's part of the dealership. Whether you decide to step in his place, sell his share, or hire someone to act in your stead, I will do all I can to make that transition as easy as possible."

Megan studied the man, but there was no evidence to suggest he had ulterior motives.

He made sure there was nothing else they needed and bid them farewell before stepping out of the office.

"So now we need to find out what happened to all the money that he received from selling half of the dealership plus what he got from the second mortgage..." Gabe began.

Megan finished the thought. "...and find his will to see exactly what he intended to do with it all." She glanced at Mom. "It's got to be at the house. Tonight, we search from top to bottom until we find it."

The office door opened slowly, and Helen peeked in. "I'm so sorry to interrupt, but I wanted to see if you all needed more coffee. Or something to eat."

"No, thank you," Mom said as she stood. "We're

heading back to the house. We have a long night of searching ahead of us."

Helen nodded in compassion. "I'll be working here until after six. How about I come by and help you look? I could order in some dinner for us. Or at least keep the coffee brewing."

Mom stepped around the desk and gave her a hug. "That's kind, Helen. Thank you."

As they put files back where they belonged and gathered their things, Megan sent a text to Bryce.

> "We didn't find the will, but we learned a lot. I'll call and update soon."

She wished she could talk to him in person instead. Funny how she'd become so used to it.

It didn't take long for his reply to appear.

> "I look forward to hearing from you."

"Wow," Bryce said after hearing how Megan's day went. She'd surprised him by suggesting they chat through video if he had a few minutes. He was sitting on one of the bunks in the small dorm where he could get some privacy. "How'd your mom take the news about him selling half the dealership?"

"I'm not sure." The sound of papers shuffling filled the background. "She'll probably need to process it, and it may be that she needs to find the will and see what Dad wanted to do first, you know?"

"It seems odd to me that your dad might have a will that your mom knows nothing about. That they didn't draw one up together." He knew his parents had a financial advisor that they spoke to and a will they updated every few years. He couldn't imagine his parents keeping secrets from each other—certainly not related to their finances.

"Yeah, me, too." She glanced behind her at the closed door he could barely see on screen.

"Which room are you talking in?"

"One of the spare rooms. Mom always had it set up as a craft room, though I don't recall her ever using it." Megan turned the camera away from her and panned around the room. It was neat, tidy, and mostly empty. When her face reappeared, she asked, "How are things going there?"

"It's been quiet so far. We've been going over some drills. There's a new guy coming in, so he dropped by for a while." He paused. "I wish I were there helping you search."

"I wish you were, too." She lowered her voice. "I don't know how long this is going to take. Gabe headed back to the station after he made sure we got here safely. Someone else is keeping watch outside. I think Helen is coming by to help for a while." There was a hesitation in her voice.

Bryce read between the lines. If the search took long enough, she might have to stay the night there, something he knew she didn't want to do. It killed him that he wasn't at the house as well, offering what comfort he could. "No matter what time of the night you get done, you can call the station, and someone will make sure you get back to my parents' house."

"I appreciate that. I did call and let your parents know I wouldn't be there for dinner, and that I'd update them later in the evening."

"Megan? What happened there that week before graduation?" The moment the words were out of his mouth,

Bryce wished he'd kept them to himself. "I'm sorry, I shouldn't have asked."

She shook her head, the camera moving back and forth with the motion. "No. You have a right to know." Megan studied something off camera, whether it was in the room with her or in the past, Bryce didn't know. "Everything about my father centered around manipulation. He used his dealership and the relationships he made around town to influence what others thought of him. Here at the house... He used my mom and me to control each other."

Bryce had assumed as much but hearing her say it made his blood boil. He held his tongue and provided her the time she needed to continue.

Megan gave him a look that melded an apology with shame. "My father hated you and your family. I truly never knew if he had a problem with your parents at one point, or if it's because you and I ... because we got along, and I didn't ask for his permission to see you. I had to cancel dates with you so many times because he decided I needed to work on something at home at the last moment, or he chose to punish me for something that would normally slide by."

Bryce had known her father didn't care for him, and he'd even spoken to his own dad about it. At the time, all he could do was his best, be polite, and hope her parents came around. Knowing what he did now, he doubted that ever would've happened. "I'm sorry."

She shrugged. "He wanted me to go into accounting and come work for the dealership. I'd told him for years it wasn't something I was interested in. I don't think he wanted it to stay in the family so much as have a way to control me once I was an adult." Megan slowly released a lungful of air. "I think he knew you and I were getting seri-ous. I'd mentioned our plans of going to college together. He was probably afraid I was going to tell you the truth about him."

She paused again. With a quick glance at something off screen, Megan continued. "That week before graduation, he told me that I either needed to attend the community college here in Destiny or go to work with him at the dealership. If I didn't choose one of those two options, he'd have to take matters into his own hands." Megan's voice broke. "When I told him I had no intention of doing either of those, he backhanded me." She swallowed hard and put a hand to her cheek as though she could still feel the pain.

"Megan..." Bryce's heart ached for her as much as his anger sparked toward her father.

"Mom started crying then, and I remember my father smiling as he watched me." She shuddered. "That's when I told him that I was leaving town. The only way I could see anything changing is if I made it impossible for him to manipulate me any longer." Her gaze focused on the phone again. "I turned to Mom and asked her to go with me."

Bryce's eyes widened. He hadn't expected that. "She refused."

Megan nodded. "My father looked so triumphant. Bryce, I begged her to stand up to him and leave, but she chose to stay. I knew then that she would never walk away, and I couldn't continue to watch him abuse her like he did. I promised myself that day that I would never spend another night in this house."

So much of what happened that week made sense now. Bryce thought back to what Gabe had said at the precinct once he'd heard of Mr. Bristow's tendencies. He agreed—it was probably good finding him and making him regret the way he put Megan through hell as a child was no longer an option. He cursed, then apologized for his language. "It makes me angry that he never had to pay for what he did to you and your mom." Someone came into the dorm, and Bryce gave the guy a wave and waited for him to leave before continuing. "I wish I'd known what you were going through."

Tears filled her eyes. "If I hadn't left, he would've held that over my head. Bryce, if we'd stayed together, he would've made our lives miserable. It was the only way I could break away so he no longer had a hold on me." Her eyes slid closed, and it was several moments before her long lashes lifted again. "Your home was here—your family, friends. And I knew I wouldn't be back so long as my father was still living. I couldn't ask that of you, too." A tear escaped, then and slid down her cheek. "I left because I cared too much about you to drag things out. And look where we are now. You've done amazing things with your life, Bryce."

He swallowed his objection. He wanted to tell her that he'd have left town with her in a heartbeat, or that they would've figured it out. Maybe they could've gone to the police about what her father was doing. But in the end, he knew she'd done her best with what she had. Looking back and rehashing it changed nothing. "You have no idea how badly I want to be there to hold you right now."

The corners of her mouth lifted a little as she swiped away another tear. "You and me both."

"You're going to find that will tonight, Megan. We're going to catch whoever is trying to hurt you and your mom. Then before you go home, we're going to talk." He refused to let her walk away again. He didn't know what that meant for his future or hers yet, but if he had anything to say about it, they'd be together.

"I sure hope you're right." She brushed some hair out of

her face. "I'd probably better get back out there and help. Mom's got a system in place." One eyebrow lifted, insinuating she wasn't so sure about her mother's methods.

Bryce chuckled. "I'll bet she does. And Megan..." He'd almost told her he loved her but stopped himself at the last minute. Because when he told her that again, he wanted it to be in person. "...be careful."

"I will. You, too."

Chapter Eighteen

One of the first things they did when they returned to the house was pull out the boxes her father had stored at the back of his office closet. The number of boxes they still needed to go through was dwindling. Megan was nearly going cross-eyed looking at all the fine print on the documents she'd unearthed. And still none of them were what they were looking for. How could her father, who was so organized at work with his clients, be so seemingly disorderly at home?

Maybe it wasn't so much that he was unorganized as that he seemed to have kept every single piece of paper that he had ever received. Had he wanted to make sure he had something documented just in case? Or was it more of a hoarding situation? Megan supposed she'd never know now, not that it really made much of a difference.

She made a mental note to be sure she went through all her belongings and paperwork so that her kids didn't have to once she passed. Many, many years in the future, of course. Assuming she got married. Or had kids.

Not for the first time that evening, Megan's thoughts

shifted to Bryce. With the exception of the time they were in high school talking about a possible future together, she'd been content with the idea of never marrying.

The whole adage about women marrying men who are like their fathers? That scared Megan so badly that she figured it was better to never marry at all.

Except Bryce was about as opposite from her father as you could get. Not that she was thinking about marriage with him. But *if*—and that was a big if—she ever got married, it'd be to someone like him.

Someone who put his family first. Who risked his life to save others.

The kind of man his wife and kids could be proud of.

Megan thought about the last things Bryce had said to her on their video call before she had to hang up. He said he wanted to talk.

He'd told her the other day that he wanted to stay in touch after she went back home. There was a large part of her that hoped he might want to get back together again. What that would look like, she didn't know. She was too exhausted tonight to even try to imagine how that would work.

But fear kept pushing its way to the surface. A whisper in the back of her mind insisted he'd see her differently now that he knew what a horrible person her dad was.

Megan could look at Bryce's parents and easily see how he became the amazing man he was.

Would he look at hers and be worried about the kind of wife or mother she might be in the future?

The unsettling thought had her frowning as she stared, unseeing, at a file in her hands.

The doorbell sounded, and Megan was relieved to focus on something else.

Mom stood from the desk chair with a groan. "Oh, thank goodness. That must be Helen. We could use another set of eyes."

Megan jumped up from her spot on the floor. "Hold on, Mom. Let me go with you. We need to make sure it's her at the door." A police officer was supposed to be sitting outside, but you couldn't be too careful. Knowing Mom, she'd just throw the door open and think about it later.

Downstairs, Megan looked through the peephole. Helen was standing on the other side, a police officer beside her.

Megan opened the door. "We were expecting her," she told the officer who gave a nod of satisfaction. Megan ushered the woman in.

Mom met Helen with a hug. "Thank you so much for coming by."

"You're welcome. I'm just glad I can help in some way. Let me put in a quick call for delivery. Does pizza sound good?" When they agreed, Helen continued. "I offered to order something for the nice young officer out front—he was in his car when I arrived—but he said he's not allowed to accept food while on duty." Helen looked disappointed. "I'll be sure to get enough to have leftovers, which is never a bad thing." She waved them away. "You go on back upstairs. I'll place the order, grab us some fresh tea, and I'll be there in a minute."

Mom smiled and led the way to the office. "Pizza sounds wonderful. I can't remember the last time I had it."

Helen rejoined them a short time later, a tray containing three glasses of tea in her hands and her purse over one shoulder. "Thirty minutes for delivery," she said. "That's not too bad."

"It'll give us time to go through some more paperwork."

Mom said, taking a drink of her tea. "I'm just so thankful for your help. Megan and I have been searching all evening."

"I take it you haven't had any luck?"

"Not yet."

Megan only half listened to their conversation. She sent a text to Bryce to let him know Helen had arrived, and that they hadn't found anything useful yet. When he didn't respond a few minutes later, she tucked her phone away again. Was he on a call out? She said a silent prayer for his safety if that were the case.

Mom put Helen to work looking through another box while she sorted a stack of folders she'd started on earlier.

Megan had just finished a box, so she packed it back up and stacked it on top of some others in the corner. There were no other boxes to tackle.

Megan stood in the center of the room, hands on her hips, and looked around. Where else could her father hide something? Her gaze roamed the boxes, traveled over the desk, and stalled at the two file cabinets.

Something didn't seem quite right about one of them, but she couldn't figure out what. She glanced over her shoulder at Mom who was by the desk looking through things and Helen sitting on one of the plush chairs going through an accordion folder. Both women were completely preoccupied as they talked about the fall festival coming up.

Megan got closer to the cabinets and sat on the floor. There was space between the bottom drawer of each and the floor. But for the cabinet on the left, the space was at least three inches taller.

She ran a finger along the base but didn't feel anything. She pulled the bottom drawer out just a few inches and felt along the top of that space and slightly behind.

There!

An indent snagged her attention. She pressed a finger into it and heard a click. Megan gasped when the bottom drawer slid in, and the newly-discovered, much shallower drawer below it popped out. It resembled a safe deposit box with several manila envelopes nestled inside.

Megan withdrew the small stack. She opened the first one and read "Last Will and Testament" at the top. Her heart raced.

"I found the will!" Megan lifted the manila envelope above her head. "There's something else here, too."

She put the will on the floor and opened the next envelope. It looked like information about her parents' vehicles.

The last envelope held what appeared to be deed information about not only her parents' home, but the dealership as well. Judging from the legalese, they would need a lawyer to help them go over everything.

Mom and Helen dropped what they were looking at to sit on the floor by Megan. Mom reached for the deed to the house and pulled it out of the envelope. She quickly read it and released a relieved sigh. "Okay, Richard and I are both listed. I was starting to worry that maybe only his name was on there. I still need to get the second mortgage issue managed, but this makes me feel a little better."

Megan was happy for her mom. Hopefully, they could figure out where all the money had gone, pay the second mortgage, and Mom would get her house back.

"What about the dealership?" Helen asked as Megan handed the file to Mom.

Mom perused the front page like Megan had and looked as equally perplexed. "It's the same paperwork Gary showed us earlier." She turned to the second page and then the third. "Yes, it also shows Richard owning half of the dealership and Gary the other half, just like he told us." She tapped the paper. "I didn't doubt him, but it's good to have our own copy."

Helen held out a hand for the file. "I'm used to reading a lot of legal mumbo jumbo over there. Let me look at it. Why don't you glance at the will. Make sure everything is all lined out there. That will make a difference."

Mom nodded and handed it over. She picked up the envelope containing the will and stared at it for several moments in silence. She wiped a tear from her cheek and started to open it. Her eyes traveled the words on the front page, she flipped that over, and continued to read, her brows drawing together. "I don't understand..."

"What is it?" Megan leaned closer, trying to see what had her mom confused.

"It says here that he's making sure the house goes to me. But our savings account... Part goes to me, and part goes to..." She stopped and looked at Helen with wide eyes. "To Leroy Gadd." Mom looked between the paper and Helen. "Who's Leroy? Is he related to you? Why would Richard be leaving him money?"

Megan wasn't surprised that he hadn't listed her in the will. She didn't want any of his money, anyway. But it still stung—like it was that last nail in the coffin of what might have been a proper father and daughter relationship. Suddenly, Mom's words sank in. "What? There's nothing left in the savings account, according to the bank. But even if there were, why—"

"Forget the savings account—what does it say about his share of the dealership?" Helen snatched the will away. "This is impossible!" Her words, spoken loudly and with a sneer, echoed off the walls. "He said he'd leave the dealership to Leroy."

Megan, annoyed at the fact that Helen seemed to be

trying to weasel her way into the situation, took the will back from her. "That makes no sense. I get that he might not leave it to me, but it sounds like he left it to Mom which is as it should be."

"You have no idea." Helen scrambled to her feet. "Neither of you have a clue, do you?" She laughed, her voice matching the anger flashing in her eyes. She jabbed a finger at Mom. "For years, he said he couldn't leave you because it would sully his good name and the business. But he would make sure our son was taken care of."

The sadness on Mom's face made Megan's heart ache. "You two had an affair." There was no accusation in Mom's voice, just acceptance. Had she known all along, or was she simply not surprised at what her husband might do?

Helen cocked her head to the side, a satisfied look on her face. "He only stayed with you because he felt sorry for you. And because he didn't want the town talking. Leroy is our son, and it's time to go public so that Leroy can take over what's rightfully his." She turned her attention on Megan. "After all, you clearly weren't interested. Leroy has as much right to your father's business as you do." Her expression changed again, into something piercing. Scary. "We've waited a long time for this moment, and a piece of paper isn't going to change a thing."

Helen snatched the will and took several steps back. Megan moved to stop her, but Helen reached into her purse and took out a small handgun. Without hesitation, she aimed it at Mom. "You take another step, and I'm ending this right now." She smirked at Mom. "You've been a thorn in my side for years."

Helen shifted her gun from Mom to Megan and back. "Push those other envelopes over here."

Not seeing much choice, Megan used her foot to kick

them in her direction. "What are you planning to do? You're not going to be able to change what's in the will."

"Maybe not. But it wasn't filed with an attorney. Which means, if it simply disappears, and the two of you are taken care of, then it'll be hard for anyone to contest that Leroy is the right person to inherit the dealership."

Megan's heart lodged in her throat. "It was Leroy who set the fire at the hotel and tried to shoot me. Wasn't it?"

"And if he'd taken care of you in the beginning like I told him to, I wouldn't be here cleaning up his mess."

It made sense now why he'd sabotaged so many escape ladders. He probably hadn't known which room Megan would be staying in when she arrived, so he compromised all that were empty at the time. Which meant he'd been watching her since she'd first driven into Destiny. The thought sent a shudder up her spine.

Megan motioned to the paperwork. "Look, take everything and leave. Trust me when I say I want no part of the dealership. As far as I'm concerned, Leroy can have it all." She'd say whatever she needed to if it would help defuse the situation. She thought about the phone in her back pocket but feared reaching for it would cause Helen to lose what little control she still had. "You don't need to hurt anyone here."

"Want? Need? It's a fine line." Helen raised her voice. "Leroy!"

Shuffling at the office door snagged Megan's attention. A tall, gangly man a little younger than her stood in the doorway. "Surprise." He grinned, his front teeth darkened or missing. "It's nice to meet you, *sis*." He spat on the carpet after the last word.

Panic rose like bile in Megan's throat. How had he

gotten past the officer out front and into the house? Was the officer okay? *God, please, protect us. Send help.*

Mom shrank and grasped Megan's hand with a strength Megan didn't know she possessed. "It's going to be okay, Mom."

"I wouldn't make promises you can't keep," Helen snarled. "You two, get in the closet."

Megan hooked her arm through Mom's and pulled her closer, angling herself so that she was between Mom and the duo in front of them. "You don't need to do this. I'm sure we can figure everything out."

"There's nothing to figure out." Helen's eyes were wide now—almost wild. "Richard chose Wendy over me. My boy has missed out all his life. I'm going to make sure he gets what he deserves." She used her weapon to motion them toward the closet again.

Leroy took a gun out of the waistband of his pants, a grin on his face. "Come on, in you go."

Megan led Mom to the closet and followed her inside. "What are you going to do?"

Helen closed them in with a slam of the closet doors. "Nothing you need to worry about." Her words dripped with hatred and sarcasm.

Megan blinked against the darkness. Some light came in through the cracks around the doors. Her eyes adjusted quickly, and she focused on the activity in the room beyond.

"Move it over there. Quick."

They heard something heavy being dragged across the floor. Megan could only imagine it was the huge, mahogany desk. They were probably moving it in front of the closet doors. There'd be no way she could push it out of the way from inside.

Panic took hold, and Megan's heart began to race. She

wanted to shake the doors. Push them open. But with two armed people in the next room, it wouldn't do her or Mom any good.

Wait, her phone!

Megan grabbed it out of her back pocket, thankful that Helen had been far too angry to think about confiscating it. She didn't dare call in case they heard her talking, so she muted her phone and sent a text to Bryce.

> "It's Helen. She has us at gunpoint at Mom's house. Two people, two guns. I don't know if the officer is okay or not."

Hopefully, the message would go through, and Bryce would call it in with the police department.

Finally, all sounds from the other side of the room faded. Megan could hear their two captors descend the stairs followed by more talking. Megan couldn't quite figure out what they were saying, though.

Mom put a hand to her chest and leaned against the jackets on her side of the closet. "I'm sorry, Megan. I'm sorry you got dragged into the middle of this."

"It's not your fault, Mom." Megan looked at her mom, studied her face. "Did you know Dad was cheating?" Mom's hesitation spoke volumes. "Why didn't you say something? Or leave him? You deserved better than that." They both deserved better than what her father had had to offer.

"It's not that easy." Mom shook her head sadly. "Where would I have gone? What was I supposed to do? I refused to live in squalor while he lived well when I'm the one who helped him get there in the first place."

Megan didn't miss that it was all about the money and didn't seem to have anything to do with loving him.

"Did you know it was Helen?"

Tears sprang to Mom's eyes as she shook her head. "I thought we were friends."

If Leroy was truly his son, that meant he'd been cheating on Mom long before Megan ever left town. The thought sickened her.

Yet, somehow, she wasn't surprised.

Sad.

She could still hear voices downstairs. A few minutes later, someone came back up to the office. Megan heard something metallic, an odd sound she couldn't quite place, and then shuffling again as the person left. Seconds later, the front door slammed shut. The silence that followed was quickly punctuated by a shrill noise.

Mom gripped Megan's arm. "It's the smoke alarm," she said, her voice high.

Megan paused and took a tentative whiff. Smoke and something else. Was that gasoline? Panic started to set in.

Helen and Leroy had set the house on fire.

Bryce had just finished checking inventory when his phone rang. "Hey, Gabe. Any news?"

"Yep." Shuffling sounds in the background made it sound like he was walking somewhere. "You remember when we said we'd get a list of the juveniles who had been arrested for starting fires and compare that to individuals still living in Destiny? Well, we got a hit for one Leroy Gadd. I did a little digging and take a wild guess who he's related to."

The last name sounded familiar, but Bryce couldn't quite place it. "Tell me."

"Helen   Gadd—Mr.   Bristow's   assistant   at   the dealership."

Dread pooled in Bryce's belly. "Gabe..."

"I also contacted the company that was sending the foreclosure notices to Mrs. Bristow. They deposited that money in a specific account that Mr. Bristow had given them. A bank account in Leroy's name."

"Gabe! Helen's supposed to go over to the Bristow home to help them search for the will this evening if she's not already there."

Something slammed in the background. "I'm already on it."

Bryce's phone dinged with a text. "Hold on." He opened the text and read,

> "It's Helen. She has us at gunpoint at Mom's house. Two people, two guns. I don't know if the officer is okay or not."

He relayed the message to Gabe. "Go, go!"

The moment he hung up, his phone rang again. As soon as he saw Megan's name, he answered it so quickly he nearly dropped the phone. "Megan? Are you okay?"

"Bryce, listen. It's Helen and her son. She had an affair with my dad. They just left, but they're trying to burn the evidence. They set the house on fire." She coughed. "Mom and I are barricaded in the closet in my dad's office. I can't get the doors open." There was no missing the panic in her voice.

Bryce wrote the address on a piece of paper, handed it to Menendez and mouthed, "Fire in progress. Megan's trapped." Menendez jumped up and immediately sounded the alarm. "Get as close to the floor as you can, cover your mouth and nose, and hang in there. Megan, I'm coming for you."

They'd been dispatched and were on their way in minutes. Now, as they raced to the Bristow home, all he could do was pray that they got there in time.

When Bryce got his first look at the house, it was already engulfed in flames. Helen had to have used an accelerant to get it this fully involved so quickly. Bryce clenched his fists. Helen and her son better hope Gabe got to them first.

He jumped out of the truck to see that Gabe and several other squad cars had already arrived. Gabe jogged down the sidewalk toward him. "Officer Krautscheid was watching the house. We just found him stabbed in the front seat of the squad car, but he still has a pulse. He's on his way to the hospital." He clenched his teeth. "We're searching for Helen and Leroy now." He stalled. "Where's Megan?"

"They trapped her and Mrs. Bristow inside." He checked his gear as they talked.

Gabe's eyes widened slightly before they narrowed again. "You focus on them, and I'll take care of Helen and her son."

They shook hands and Bryce clapped him on the shoulder. "Be careful."

"You, too!" Gabe hollered as he hurried away.

Their chief barked out orders. Like a well-oiled machine, Bryce and his company got into positions, some of them working the hose to start dousing the flames while Bryce and three others readied for their trek inside the house.

"Once through the front door, there's a staircase to the right. Follow it, turn right again, and that's the office. Megan and her mother are being held inside that closet. There's a piece of furniture in front of the doors."

They nodded their understanding. Menendez stepped in front of Bryce. "I need you to stay focused, Keyes. Can you do that?"

"Yes, sir." Bryce wasn't going to rest until they got the two women out safely.

"Let's do this."

Bryce gave a single nod, put his mask over his face, made sure the others were ready, and they charged inside.

He knew exactly where to go, but it always amazed him how different a building can look when smoke and the eerie yellow and gold light from the fire filled the space. All four of them reached the office and efficiently moved the desk away from the closet doors.

As soon as Bryce flung them open, he was relieved to see Megan still alert. She and Mrs. Bristow had jackets pressed against their mouths and were lying on the floor of the closet.

Thank you, Lord.

One of Bryce's mates didn't hesitate. He lifted Mrs. Bristow and carried her downstairs, followed by his partner.

Bryce placed an arm around Megan's shoulders. "You ready?"

She nodded, her eyes on his. He shifted so that his arm went around her waist before quickly leading her out of the office, his partner right behind him.

Fire burned brightly around them as he helped maneuver the stairs. The moment they burst through the front door, he felt Megan take a deep breath before he heard it. Immediately, violent coughs had her doubled over.

Bryce escorted Megan to the waiting ambulance. Her mother was already being attended to. Curtis looked up and motioned for Megan to take a seat. "We've got to stop meeting like this," he joked.

Megan coughed and nodded, amusement in her watery eyes. "I agree."

Bryce touched her shoulder. "I need to help get this fire out."

She placed a hand on his. "I'm good," she croaked. "Go."

It took some time to get the fire under control. It was clear, between the speed at which the fire had engulfed the house, and from Megan's report, that Helen had used gas to get it going. He hadn't received an update from Arnold or Gabe, not that he'd had much time to check. Hopefully, they had no problem catching her and her son.

When the fire was nearly out, Bryce stood back and surveyed the damage. It would take time and an inspection, but he had serious doubts that the home could be salvaged. His heart ached for Mrs. Bristow, especially, who may be dealing with the loss of her home so soon after the death of her husband.

After making sure that the chief didn't need him for anything else, he took his helmet off and scanned the street, looking for Megan. The ambulance was gone, and his heart sank.

"They took them to the hospital for smoke inhalation," Chief Menendez told him.

Chapter Nineteen

For the second time in a week, Bryce burst into the emergency room and strode to the front desk. "I'm looking for Megan Bristow. She was just brought in for smoke inhalation."

The woman manning the front desk took in his uniform, checked her computer, and pointed down the hall. "Room 108."

"Thank you," he said with a slap of his palm against the countertop. He ran down the hall and skid to a stop at the correct room. The door was partly closed, and he pushed it open slowly. "Megan?"

He spotted her lying on the hospital bed, an oxygen mask over her nose and mouth. As soon as she saw him, her eyes brightened, and she tried to sit up.

The nurse with her put a hand out to stop her. "I need you to relax for a few more minutes." She motioned for Bryce to come on in.

He strode across the room and took Megan's hand in his. He looked at the nurse. "Is she going to be okay?"

The nurse looked from him to Megan. "Is it okay to fill

him in?" Upon Megan's nod, she continued, "Miss Bristow has suffered minor smoke inhalation. We're giving her some oxygen, going to run a few blood tests, but overall, she's a very lucky woman."

"Praise God," he said, drawing Megan's hand to his mouth and kissing it. "And her mother?"

"She's a couple doors down, but she will be fine, too."

Bryce rubbed circles across the top of Megan's hand with his thumb while they waited for the nurse to observe Megan's oxygen level. She seemed satisfied with the numbers, lifted the oxygen mask, and offered Megan some water to drink.

"I'm going to check on your mom while we wait for your blood test results. I'll be back."

With that, she left the room, closing the door behind her.

Bryce reached over and gently smoothed Megan's hair away from her eyes, running a finger down her cheek. "You've got to quit scaring me like this." He leaned in and brushed her lips with his. The relief of seeing her safe, combined with the adrenaline of nearly losing her, created a heady combination. When she didn't move to withdraw, he kissed her again, slowly, thoroughly.

She broke the kiss, turning her head to the side to cough. "Sorry," she said, her cheeks pink and eyes glossy.

"No, you're fine. You're okay." He sat on the edge of the hospital bed. When she leaned her head against his shoulder, a soft sigh escaped. He soaked in the feel of her taking steady breaths, his own heart rate slowly returning to normal. "We're okay."

"Bryce, I..."

"Look, Megan..."

They both laughed when they realized they'd spoken at the same time.

The door opened again with a knock. Gabe peeked around the corner and grinned. "Hey, you two. I'm glad to see you both alive and kicking." He gave Megan a hug and shook Bryce's hand. "I wanted to tell you personally that we located Helen and Leroy. They gave us a bit of a chase, but they lost control of their vehicle and rolled it at the edge of town."

"Did they make it?" Megan asked.

Gabe grunted and lowered his voice. "Somehow. We have them in custody now. They still had the guns in their possession, the car smelled like gasoline, and the paperwork they stole from your mother was strewn across the back-seat." He grinned. "They'll be in prison for a long time."

Megan visibly relaxed into Bryce.

"How's Krautscheid?"

"He's in surgery now, but the doctor said, if all goes well, he should make a full recovery."

"It's over?" Megan's voice was soft, vulnerable.

"It's over." Bryce focused on her again, dipping down to kiss her lips.

"Hey, you guys, get a room," Gabe interrupted.

Megan chuckled and ducked her chin.

Bryce gave his friend a serious look. "Dude, if you don't like the view, the door's right over there."

When Megan awoke the next morning, sunshine poured through the window at the Keyes' home. She looked at the clock resting on the small side table and gasped. It was nearly noon.

She sat up with a start. When was the last time she'd slept nearly twelve hours? Not since she'd gone through residency as a nurse. It was no wonder, though, after everything she'd been through lately. She supposed, with the danger gone and Helen and Leroy caught, she was finally able to relax.

A smile tugged at the corners of her mouth as she thought about Bryce. He'd refused to leave her side until they'd gotten back to his parents' house, and even then, it was under protest.

She swallowed, and the scratchy feel of her throat made her cough. She took a long drink from the glass of water on the side table. Dealing with smoke inhalation for the second time in a week had left her throat incredibly irritated.

She glanced at her phone. She touched the screen to see she had a voicemail from Janet along with texts from Paige. Wow, she must have been dead to the world last night if notifications and a phone call hadn't awakened her.

She responded to Paige's text to let her know she was good and would call her later. Then she listened to Janet's voicemail.

"Hey, Megan. I hope your mother is doing okay. Smokey is well, though I think he's becoming bored with me. I'm sure he'll be glad to see you when you get back. Hey, I wanted to give you a heads up. I'm getting pressure from the powers that be to hire more nurses to replace anyone who can't work full shifts... I'd really hate to lose you. But I'm going to need to get you back on the schedule as soon as possible. Give me a call with an update when you can, okay?"

Megan called her and reassured her she'd head home tomorrow morning and be at work that evening for the night shift. Which meant she had less than twenty-four hours to spend in Destiny. It was a fact that would have had her doing cartwheels of joy less than a week ago. But now...

A soft knock on her door was followed by Mrs. Keyes' voice. "Megan, honey, are you awake?"

Megan grabbed the small, crocheted blanket folded at the end of the bed and pulled it around her shoulders. She opened the door a crack and peeked out. "Yes, but only just now," Megan said, her voice strained. She coughed and cleared her throat. "I'm so sorry. I seriously overslept." Hopefully, her scratchy voice would return to normal in a day or two.

"I'm glad—you needed it." She smiled kindly. "I hesitated to wake you, but Gabe has stopped by with some updates, and I thought you'd want to hear firsthand."

"Yes, definitely. Thank you so much, I'll be right down." Megan smiled at her and shut the door again. She rushed through getting dressed then cleaned up in the bathroom. She glanced down the hall to see that the door to Bryce's room was closed.

He should have been done with his shift. She promised him she'd say goodbye before she left town again, and she had every intention of keeping it.

Her heart heavy, she made her way to the kitchen where the delicious scent of tacos had her stomach growling. "It smells amazing in here," she said, trying to keep her voice upbeat as she accepted a hug from Mrs. Keyes.

"I wish I could take credit for making these myself, but a certain son of mine brought them over," Mrs. Keyes said, her eyes glittering with amusement.

A sound in the doorway brought Megan around. She spotted Bryce leaning against the doorframe, a grin on his face. "I figured I couldn't go wrong with tacos."

They walked toward each other at the same time,

meeting in the middle. She sank into his arms, resting her head against his chest, soaking in the warmth of him and the security of his embrace. Megan leaned away enough to look up at him. "I'm so glad you're here." She ducked her head and coughed into her arm.

He swept some hair off her cheek and deposited it behind her ear. "How are you feeling?"

The concern in his eyes warmed her. "I'm okay. My voice sounds worse than I feel." Megan gave Bryce a smile that she hoped would reassure him.

He hugged her tightly before releasing her again. "Good. And your mom?"

"I haven't talked to her yet today, but last night she was doing as well as could be expected. Believe it or not, she's staying at the B & B until the fire inspection is complete." It was hard to picture Mom staying anywhere besides a five-star hotel. "I was planning on checking in on her soon. I'm not sure what she's going to do in the long run."

Someone at the table cleared his throat dramatically. They turned to find Gabe gesturing to the platter of tacos. "They aren't getting any warmer, you know," he said with a wink.

Mrs. Keyes gave him a good-natured swat on the arm. "Hush, now."

Bryce laughed and guided Megan to the table where they sat across from Gabe. Mr. and Mrs. Keyes joined them. After a prayer of thanks covering the events of the last few days, everyone echoed a heartfelt "amen." Tacos were passed around along with glasses of tea or soda.

Megan took a long drink, thankful for the cool liquid against her throat. Her tea had the perfect amount of sugar. "This tastes so good. Thank you."

"Of course." Without hesitating, Mrs. Keyes refilled her glass with a smile.

They ate for several minutes before Gabe began sharing news from the investigation. "Once we had Helen and Leroy in different interrogation rooms, Leroy raced to tell us everything." He raised an eyebrow. "To make a long story short, Helen was blackmailing Mr. Bristow, telling him that if he provided for both her and Leroy, she'd stay quiet. But as time went on, she kept asking for more and more money."

Megan nodded slowly. "And that's why he sold half of the dealership."

"Exactly. And took out a second mortgage on the house." Gabe wiped his mouth with a napkin. "He used the money to pay for Helen's silence."

"Is there any money left?" The moment Megan voiced the question, she already knew the answer.

"Unfortunately, no." Gabe gave Megan a sympathetic look. "Leroy has an extensive gambling problem. Every bit of the money that your father gave Helen went to pay off loan sharks at one time or another."

"Which explains why Helen was becoming desperate to get her hands on more," Bryce said. He opened another taco and took a bite, chewing thoughtfully. "I wonder if Mr. Bristow ever insisted on a paternity test?"

"The court will be ordering one," Gabe assured them.

"I doubt Dad would've paid Helen a cent if he hadn't been certain that Leroy was his son," Megan said quietly. She was still having trouble grasping the fact that her father not only cheated, but that she had a half brother who had tried to kill her. "Although I really hope I'm wrong. The thought of being related..." She shivered.

Bryce covered her hand with his. "None of it has anything to do with you or who you are."

"Here, here," Gabe said in agreement.

Megan gave them a small smile. "I appreciate that." Another thought came to mind. She frowned. "How did Leroy get into the house in the first place?"

Gabe finished his glass of tea which Mrs. Keyes promptly refilled. "It turns out, when Helen stayed downstairs to order the pizza, she unlocked the front door. Leroy arrived at the house with a pizza box and came around the side of the patrol car. Since Krautscheid was expecting a delivery, he started to get out of the car. Leroy incapacitated him with a taser, then stabbed him." He shook his head angrily. "It was easy for him to get into the house from there."

"The whole situation is such a shame," Mrs. Keyes said with a click of her tongue, and Mr. Keyes agreed.

"Desperation will make people do strange things."

The table fell silent as everyone continued their meal, the air heavy with contemplation. It was a relief when Gabe interrupted it.

"Thankfully, they'll both be behind bars for a long, long time. In other news, Krautscheid made it through surgery and is already driving the nurses crazy."

Megan chuckled. "That's a good sign, then."

"That it is." Gabe took another drink of his tea, then set the glass down on the table with a thud. "Megan, do you know when you'll be heading back to San Antonio?"

She cringed. She'd hoped to break the news to Bryce first. She glanced at him then down at her hands. "Tomorrow morning."

Gabe nodded. "I thought as much." He stood. "I'd better get back to the station. You would not believe the pile of paperwork I need to fill out after all of this." He walked around and gave Megan a hug. "Don't be a stranger, okay?"

"I won't," Megan assured him, sad at the thought of leaving her friends. "Thanks for everything, Gabe."

Everyone else said their goodbyes, and Gabe left. Mrs. Keyes started clearing the table, then came back with a plate of cookies. "You kids take these out into the living room. I need to get this table cleared off and some laundry going." She gave her husband a pointed look.

Mr. Keyes stood as well. "And I've got some things I need to work on in the shop. Including a cabinet my lovely wife has been waiting for me to finish." He gave Mrs. Keyes a kiss before turning to Megan. "I'm sorry for all you've gone through, but I'm real glad we got to see you again." With that, he left the dining room.

Bryce took the plate from his mom and led the way into the living room where he set the cookies on the coffee table.

Megan didn't feel like eating anything else, but she took a cookie anyway to have something to do. The chocolate chips melted on her tongue the moment she bit into it. Then again, maybe this was exactly what she needed.

Bryce polished one off in two bites. Neither of them spoke as they stood in the living room facing each other, the silence heavy between them.

She cleared her throat. "Bryce, I..." Her voice trailed off. "I was going to tell you about San Antonio. My boss left a message for me this morning, and I need to be back as soon as possible."

"I get it, Megan. I'm glad I'll get to say goodbye to you this time." His smile didn't quite reach his eyes.

"Last time, all I wanted to do was get away from here as fast as I could." Megan swallowed hard.

Bryce took a step closer to her. "And now?" His voice was just above a whisper.

"It's not that simple." She looked down and realized she

was clutching the hem of her shirt. She intentionally dropped it. "It's proving to be a lot harder to leave than I ever thought possible."

"It's all the excitement in our little town, isn't it?" Bryce said, teasing her. He shifted closer yet. "Oh, I know, it's Peter. It'd be hard for me to leave him, too."

A giggle bubbled up. The man was totally fishing, and Megan thought it was adorable. His eyes brimmed with hope, apprehension, and love.

Love that she couldn't possibly deserve after the way she'd treated him before.

Megan tried her best to act nonchalantly. "He is a cute kid. He keeps things interesting for sure." She paused, taking in a deep breath to steady her nerves. "But it might be his uncle who's causing the most trouble."

One side of his mouth hitched up a little. He took a final step that put them toe to toe. "Why would you say that? From what I've heard, he's saved you from a burning building." He looked up as though he had to do some complicated math. "Two times, if I'm not mistaken."

Megan couldn't have kept the smile from her face if she tried. "Something like that. And I have a feeling he'll never let me forget it." She raised an eyebrow at him, then sobered. "Look, Bryce, we've only had the last week to get to know each other again. After finding out about my dad and my childhood... I know it's a lot for you to take in and consider..."

"Wait right here," Bryce said, holding her gaze for a moment before turning and walking out of the room.

Stunned, Megan stood in place, wondering where he was going. He wasn't gone a full minute before he returned, a shoebox in his hand. He held it out to her. "Before anything else is said, I need you to open this." He pushed the box into her hands and took a step back.

"What is it?" She couldn't imagine what might be inside. Confused, she lifted the lid and set it on the couch nearby. The scent of charred plastic filled her nose as she studied the contents of the box. The remnants of a wooden frame stood amidst the ashes. "I don't understand..."

And then she saw them. Five metal balls half buried beneath the frame.

"The Newton's cradle from my dad's office." Her voice caught. Seeing it before had been a physical reminder of all that her father had done throughout her childhood. Now, it was barely recognizable. A tear slid down her cheek and landed in the ashes.

"I went back to the scene this morning and saw it on the floor," Bryce explained, his voice low. "I needed you to see that it's gone, Megan. Just like your father's ability to hurt you. You're free." He paused. "No matter what you decide to do going forward, I want *you* to make that choice for yourself."

Megan set the box on the coffee table and brought both hands to her mouth, releasing a slow breath against them to steady her emotions. She sniffed and wiped away another tear. "I can't believe you did this ... Thank you." She glanced at the contents of the box once again before replacing the lid. It was time to leave it and everything it represented in the past where it belonged.

Bryce took in the closed shoebox, then focused on her. "I thought I might come to San Antonio in a few days. Get to know the area a little. Maybe see what some of the fire departments there are like..." He studied her face. "If I'm not overstepping."

His words had her heart galloping in her chest. He'd

consider going to San Antonio for her? She tried to picture him there, working for one of the big fire departments in the city. But she couldn't. He belonged here in Destiny.

And maybe now she did, too.

She shook her head. "I don't think that's a good idea."

He frowned, confusion and doubt on his face. "Megan..."

She put a hand against his chest to stop him. "There's no sense in you going there if I'm coming back in a few weeks anyway."

Bryce blinked at her. "Are you serious?"

"It won't be easy. I'll need to get a job here, first. Let my landlord know, put in my notice. Travel with a cat and a goldfish. But yeah, I'm serious." She slid her arms around his waist. "I refuse to walk away from you again, Bryce Keyes."

The corners of his mouth lifted in a slow smile. "I'm glad." He cupped the back of her head with one hand and drew her closer with the other arm. "Because I wouldn't have let you." With that, he closed the distance between them with a kiss so full of promise, it left them both breathless.

Epilogue
Six Months Later

"What do you think?" Bryce stretched his arms out toward the large field in front of them. Trees surrounded it and a few flowers dotted the wild grasses that covered the open area. It'd always been one of his favorite places on his parents' property. There was something about it that, even as a young boy, seemed almost magical.

"It's absolutely beautiful." Megan stepped forward and nestled into his side. He put an arm around her to draw her in closer. It always amazed him how perfectly she fit there.

He kissed the top of her head. "Come on, help me spread the blanket out." He'd surprised her with a picnic lunch when she'd returned from helping her mom make one last trip to her new penthouse downtown. "Did your mom get all settled?"

"She did. It's not exactly like she's slumming it," Megan laughed. "There's even a doorman. Way too much for my taste, but at least she'll be happy there."

Instead of trying to have the house rebuilt after the fire rendered it uninhabitable, Mrs. Bristow had taken the insurance money, paid off the second mortgage, and then sold the land. After that, she'd sold her share of the dealership to Strider. By the time it was all said and done, Mrs. Bristow had enough money to rent a large penthouse in one of the most expensive apartment buildings in town.

"I'm glad. I know it was hard on her, but I think the house burning down might have been one of the best things for her." He set the basket on one corner of the blanket to keep the gentle breeze from folding the corner over.

"I agree. I don't know that she would've moved on otherwise." She paused, looking out over the land nearby. "I'll bet there are all kinds of wildflowers in the spring."

Bryce nodded. "A field of them." He'd brought her out here for a reason, and was going to wait until after they'd eaten, but now seemed like the perfect time. He took in a deep breath. "This is the section of land my parents gave me when I turned eighteen." He let his statement fall without turning to see her reaction.

She stilled for several moments. "Are you thinking of building a place out here now?"

He'd imagined this moment many times over the last few months. He'd never once second-guessed his decision. But now that he was in this moment, a bundle of nerves bounced around his stomach like a mini tornado.

He turned to face her and took her hands in his. A finger skimmed over the small ridge of a scar on her palm—the only evidence that remained of her burn. "I was thinking we could build ourselves a home here." He gazed into her eyes, memorizing the way they widened slightly with surprise before softening into a love he could practically feel.

Releasing one of her hands, Bryce reached for the small box he'd kept in his pocket. He pulled it out, dropped to one knee, and opened it slowly. The white gold band and trio of petite diamonds glistened in the afternoon sun.

"Losing you years ago was one of the worst things that ever happened to me. And while I hope we never go through something like that again, I did learn one very important thing." He paused. "It reminded me to treasure every moment with you. And I intend to do that to the very best of my abilities. Megan, would you do me the honor of becoming my wife? God willing, I want nothing more than to make a lifetime of memories together."

Her eyes teared up, her smile beautiful. "There's nothing else I want more."

Grinning, Bryce slipped the ring onto her finger, stood, and pulled her into his embrace. He cupped her cheeks with his hands, soaked in the joy on her face that he knew was mirrored in his own, and kissed her with all the hope he had for their future together.

A future where beauty had been created out of the ashes.

Thank you for reading **Out of the Ashes**, the first book in the Danger in Destiny series. Be sure to grab the next book, **Frozen in Jeopardy**, to read Gabe and Paige's story!

Her routine night turns terrifying.

As the storm of the century howls through Destiny, Texas, Dr. Paige Wade remains at her clinic to care for any animals that might need assistance. Her quiet night is disrupted when a man dumps an injured dog on the doorstep just hours before Paige is attacked in the parking lot.

He's uncovering deadly connections.

A call from the local animal hospital where his friend works sends Police Officer Gabe Harrison hastening to respond. The crime seems random until someone starts stalking Paige. When Gabe and his K-9 partner, Loki, discover the man who dropped off the injured dog is now a murder victim, Gabe uncovers a link between the deceased and whoever is threatening Paige.

They are running out of time.

For years, Paige has ignored her feelings for Gabe. Working closely with him means gambling with her heart. As another winter storm approaches and the murderer becomes desperate, will the risks they take not only save her life, but give them hope for a future together?

Read Frozen in Jeopardy Today!

Want a FREE BOOK?

Sign up for Melanie D. Snitker's
newsletter and get *Fear the Shadows*,
A Danger in Destiny novella, FREE!
This is Chief Arnold Dolman's story
and is exclusive to newsletter members.

Sign up today!

Special Thanks

I want to thank all of you lovely readers for jumping into this new series with me. Your patience and encouragement has been phenomenal. I hope you enjoyed reading Bryce and Megan's story as much as I enjoyed writing it.

Doug, the last couple of years have had a whole lot of ups and downs. I'm so incredibly thankful that we got to weather those together. Thanks for always encouraging me, stepping in to make sure I have time to write, and for being my best friend. I love you!

Crystal, thanks for listening to my story ideas, reading through my early (and likely scary) draft, and for all of your helpful suggestions. Your friendship, and being able to travel this author journey together, is a true blessing.

Krista, thank you so much for your editing expertise, flexibility, and for helping me make this book the best it can be.

Special thanks to my family and friends who took the time to read through this book and helped me in more ways than I can count: Kris, Rachel, Steph, Denny, Mom, Kati, and Sandy.

I also want to mention my wonderful beta readers. Not only are you all incredibly encouraging, but you manage to catch those typos that slip through the cracks. You guys are awesome!

Thank you, Heavenly Father, for the ways you've

touched my life, especially in the last year. Your love and goodness abounds!

About the Author

Melanie D. Snitker is a *USA Today* bestselling author who writes inspirational romance and romantic suspense. She and her husband live in Texas with their two children. They share their home with three dogs and two terrariums filled with frogs, a toad, and a lizard. In her spare time, Melanie enjoys photography, reading, training her dog, playing computer games, and hanging out with family and friends.

https://www.melaniedsnitker.com/

Books by Melanie D. Snitker

Danger in Destiny

Out of the Ashes

Frozen in Jeopardy

Beneath the Surface

Caught in the Crosshairs

Brides of Clearwater

Marrying Mandy

Marrying Raven

Marrying Chrissy

Marrying Bonnie

Marrying Emma

Marrying Noel

Love's Compass Complete Series

Finding Peace

Finding Hope

Finding Courage

Finding Faith

Finding Joy

Finding Grace

Books by Melanie D. Snitker

Love Unexpected Complete Series

Safe In His Arms

Someone to Trust

Starting Anew

Healing Hearts

Calming the Storm

I Still Do

Don't Kiss Me Goodbye

Sage Valley Ranch

Charmed by the Daring Cowboy

Welcome to Romance

Fall Into Romance

A Merry Miracle in Romance

www.ingramcontent.com/pod-product-compliance
Lightning Source LLC
Chambersburg PA
CBHW020617180626
46810CB00007B/2811